‘What on earth are we quarrelling about, Emma? This is so ridiculous...’

She had never looked lovelier, he thought—anger had darkened her brown eyes and her cheeks were flushed, her hair tousled. He longed to take her in his arms.

She snatched her hand away from his. ‘I’m not quarrelling.’ Emma leaned forward and smacked her hand on the table impatiently. ‘Come on, Sean—I thought we were going to be open with each other—no secrets and all that?’

‘Very well, then,’ Sean said, grim-faced. ‘You won’t like what you’re going to hear, though...’

Judy Campbell is from Cheshire. As a teenager she spent a great year at high school in Oregon, USA, as an exchange student. She has worked in a variety of jobs, including teaching young children, being a secretary and running a small family business. Her husband comes from a medical family, and one of their three grown-up children is a GP. Any spare time—when she's not writing romantic fiction—is spent playing golf, especially in the Highlands of Scotland.

Recent titles by the same author:

THE DOCTOR'S SECRET BABY
DATING DR CARTER
THE BACHELOR DOCTOR
TEMPTING DR TEMPLETON
A HUSBAND TO TRUST

THE REGISTRAR'S SECRET

BY

JUDY CAMPBELL

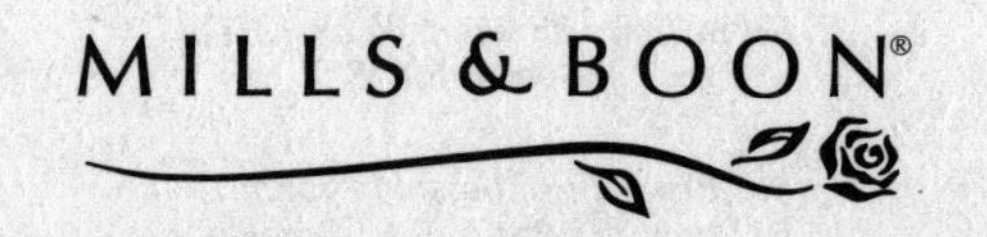

First published in Great Britain 2004
Harlequin Mills & Boon Limited,
Eton House, 18-24 Paradise Road, Richmond, Surrey TW9 1SR

ISBN 0 263 83905 2

Set in Times Roman 10½ on 12¼ pt.
03-0604-46678

Printed and bound in Spain
by Litografia Rosés, S.A., Barcelona

PROLOGUE

EMMA FULFORD peered in frustration from under her umbrella through the lashing rain at the traffic streaming past the station road. Why was it that no taxis ever came when you really, desperately needed one? She flicked a look at her watch and cursed under her breath.

'All I need, to be late on the first day of my new job—a go-slow on the trains and now a shortage of taxis,' she muttered crossly, giving a smothered yelp as a car sped past and showered her new navy trousers with dirty water.

Not quite the first impression she wanted to make—after all, she had a lot to live up to in this job, and she didn't want anyone to think that she'd been appointed just because of her connections.

Then with a sigh of thankfulness she saw a taxi responding at last to her frantic signals. It drew up with a wake of water from the puddles spraying out from either side, and Emma opened the door and sprang in, flopping back against the seat in relief. Simultaneously the door on the other side opened, and a man jumped into the far passenger seat, flinging an attaché case down between them. He leant forward towards the driver, his voice brisk.

'As quick as you can, driver. I want to go to—'

'Excuse me,' interrupted Emma coldly. 'I think I saw this taxi first, if you don't mind.'

The man turned and stared at her for a second in

surprise, rivulets of water running down his face from his rain-soaked hair.

'I didn't realise you'd got in as well,' he said curtly. 'But this is definitely my cab—I'm afraid you'll have to get out!'

Emma frowned. 'I certainly will not get out. I hailed this cab first—the driver came over to me.'

The man gave an impatient sigh. 'I've no time to argue—I've an urgent meeting to get to and I'm already late.'

The cab driver turned round in his seat and regarded both passengers sardonically through the open glass partition.

'You'd better make your minds up—I can't split the cab in two. Who's having it? I've put the clock on now—my time's money!'

Emma smiled sweetly at the man. 'Looks like you'll have to get the next cab, then, won't you? I also have an urgent appointment—and I *definitely* got this ride before you!'

The man's lips tightened stubbornly and Emma saw a flash of anger in the deep-set blue eyes he turned to her. His voice had the cold assurance of one who would get his own way in the end.

'At the risk of sounding intransigent, I repeat—this is my cab and I'd hazard a guess that my meeting is the more important.'

The driver watched them both with interest and folded his arms. 'I like a good fight,' he remarked, 'but I hope you realise it's costing you!'

Emma ignored him and fixed the other passenger with a gaze that would have terrified most men. 'Excuse me? That's one of the most arrogant comments

I've heard in my life! You've no right to make assumptions—'

The man held up his hand in a half-gesture of apology. 'OK, OK. So I was a little out of order there…but there are literally life-and-death decisions to be made at this meeting.'

What was this man like? Emma snorted derisively. 'That sounds a little melodramatic. But, as a matter of fact, my appointment could result in the same sort of decisions.'

The taxi driver gave a loud sigh. 'Well, what's it to be, then—who's going to have it?'

The man ran an impatient hand through his hair and looked angrily at Emma. 'Oh, for heaven's sake, I'm ten minutes late already. Look, where are you going to? We'll just have to share the ride, that's all—and both be late, I suppose.'

'Carrfield General Hospital…as I said, for an important appointment.'

The man lifted a surprised eyebrow 'Really? That's amazing—that's where I'm going, too! Perhaps we won't be too late after all.' His smile was sudden and unexpected and all at once he looked younger, the hard planes of his face softer. 'Not going as a patient, I hope?'

Emma wasn't going to be mollified so easily—this man had shown his true colours when he'd been thwarted.

'No—nothing like that,' she said shortly. She leaned forward and nodded to the cab driver. 'Seems we're both going to Carrfield General—so can we get a move on now?'

She subsided back in her seat and examined her fellow passenger covertly—his aquiline nose and piercing blue eyes seemed to go well with the high-handed attitude he'd shown. No doubt about it—he was good-looking in a tough, no-nonsense way, but everything about him indicated that he was the kind of man who was used to getting what he wanted, probably riding roughshod over his work colleagues. His pompous remark that his appointment was more important than hers still rankled, and his attitude reminded her only too well of dealing with another bully who had once dominated her life. Then she shrugged her shoulders. What did she care? Hopefully she wouldn't have to cross paths with this man again.

The taxi took them to the main hospital entrance, and when they got out Emma turned towards the hospital's casualty department. She nodded coolly to the man and he lifted up his hand to say farewell, glancing over her with a droll smile. The laughter in his startling blue eyes had a chancy, teasing look, as if the situation they'd found themselves in amused him.

'Perhaps we'll share a taxi again,' he remarked, his glance holding hers. 'And maybe we won't be in such a hurry next time—we'll be able to get to know each other more.'

Just for a bare nano-second Emma felt the most unbelievable flutter of excitement—an intense tingle, as if his words held some kind of dangerous promise. She almost responded with a slight smile, then gave a little shiver of distaste. How ridiculous that was! She turned away from his gaze briskly. There's no way I want to share anything again with such an arrogant man, and I certainly don't want to get to know him better, she thought grimly as she reached the doors of A and E to start the first day of her new job.

CHAPTER ONE

THERE weren't many people in the casualty waiting room at this early hour on a Monday morning—just a young girl sitting with an old lady, a man reading a newspaper and a cleaner sweeping the entrance. In a corner on the wall a large television played to a non-existent audience, its flickering image showing a woman doing a cookery demonstration, the sound a continuous low babble. Emma looked around, smiling slightly at the familiarity of the place but her mind still tingling irritably because of the encounter with her arrogant taxi companion.

She crossed over to Reception where a harassed-looking girl behind the glass was trying to fill in a form and answer a phone at the same time. She looked up enquiringly at Emma.

'Yes?' she asked, her hand over the phone's receiver.

'I'm the new registrar, Emma Fulford, doing a maternity leave locum. Dr Gorton's expecting me.'

The receptionist put down the phone and her severe expression changed to a delighted grin. 'Are we glad to see you! We weren't sure when you'd be here,' she exclaimed. 'Dr Gorton's going crazy because our specialist registrar's at a meeting and two of the nurses are off sick. Come with me and I'll spread the good news. I'm Katie, by the way—first line of defence in this madhouse!'

She set off at a trot down the corridor, and Emma followed. Dr Connie Gorton was a plump, short woman with a dishevelled appearance which went with the slightly beleaguered air of a senior registrar in a very busy department. Her round flushed face creased into a broad smile of welcome. 'Pleased to meet you, Emma—and delighted that you managed to get here. I believe there's been problems with the trains today.'

'I had a little local difficulty,' admitted Emma, as a stern face with deep blue eyes flashed into her mind. She grinned. 'Not to put too fine a point on it, I had to assert my authority over a rather obnoxious man in order to get a taxi!'

'Good for you!' Connie smiled. 'Now, this may seem a familiar scenario for A and E, but we're short-staffed, the roof in the small theatre's leaking badly and we're expecting an RTA to arrive any time—so you're doubly welcome. I know you didn't work in this department when you were here before, but I hope you'll enjoy it.'

'I'm looking forward to it and ready for anything.'

Connie pointed Emma in the direction of the staff-room behind the glassed-off reception area. 'I'll meet you in there in a minute and introduce you to the staff that are here. You'll find some hospital greens on the table to change into.'

Emma took off her soaking coat and hung it on one of the pegs of the line behind the door, glancing at herself in a small mirror hung crookedly above the sink. She grimaced. Her damp hair was beginning to dry into the springy auburn curls that always needed a strong brush to restrain them, and her nose was shiny. She pulled a comb through her hair and dabbed at her nose with powder from her compact, then pulled on the green trousers and top that were worn in this casualty department. It felt strange to be back where she'd worked three years ago—she'd never thought she'd return to Carrfield again after the fraught circumstances of her leaving.

She'd heard the job was going from an old colleague and, because it was a temporary position, she'd only seen the hospital manager when applying for the job. It suited her not to be too committed.

She gazed out of the window which looked across a large courtyard to the main hospital—a sprawling building that had had many additions since it had been built in the Edwardian era on the cliff looking over the sea. She could see the long wing of the cardiac department where her father had worked for so many years. His strong personality had left its mark, and his hard work and dedication had led to the wing being named the Fulford Wing in his memory. He had been the Grand Old Man of the hospital and very much respected in his day.

Now Professor Fulford had died and Emma had come back to give her mother moral support. A picture flew into Emma's mind of her father's public persona—charming but steely—and the very different image he'd presented to his family at home as a bully who'd exerted his authority with a tongue like a whiplash. Her mother had been the perfect example of a put-upon wife who'd kowtowed to her husband's every whim. Emma had admired her father—was proud of the way he'd risen from a deprived background to be an eminent consultant in his own field—but she had scorned the way he'd treated her mother.

I could never be tied down in a relationship with a man like my father, she thought grimly as she turned away from the window.

Rapid steps and voices could be heard coming towards the door and Connie returned, followed by two nurses, one female, the other male, and a studious-looking young man.

'A quick introduction,' she said. 'Sister Tania Cornish and Staff Nurse Bill Taylor. And this is Bob Leeming, our senior house officer. Meet our new registrar, everyone—Emma Fulford. No need to say how glad we are to see her here!'

Tania gave a friendly grin. 'You've come in the nick of time,' she said. 'The weather's causing havoc on the roads and a coach filled with football supporters has had an accident. Looks like you'll be thrown in at the deep end, Emma.'

As if to emphasise this, the standby phone rang shrilly on the wall by the door. Connie answered it briskly.

'A and E here, Dr Gorton speaking. Yes, I've noted that. Five males with minor injuries, one man being stretchered—alert but in pain. We're ready for you.'

She replaced the receiver and looked round at the enquiring faces in front of her. 'That's the coach accident,' she said. 'I'm glad to say it doesn't sound as major as I thought it might be. Seems it's a coachload of football supporters coming back from the South after a jolly weekend.'

Bill sighed gloomily. 'I always rely on a quiet Monday morning to recover from the weekend,' he groaned. 'I like to build up slowly.'

Already the sound of an ambulance's siren could be

heard coming up the drive to the hospital and then whining down to silence in front of Casualty. They all walked quickly to the doors, which slid open as a trolley was pushed through at speed. Muffled groans from under an oxygen mask came from the man on the trolley, and there were multiple cuts and abrasions on his face and arms.

'This is Bert Foley,' said the paramedic. 'Obs seem stable enough, BP 115 over 85, pulse a little fast at 110, but he's in a lot of pain round his ribs.'

Connie went over to assess the patient. Behind him, three or four staggering figures covered with thick mud made their way through the doors, laughing uproariously and singing a lewd song, each one supported by a paramedic. The nursing staff looked at each other with raised eyebrows.

Bill regarded them lugubriously. 'They certainly don't look badly injured to me—seems more like an alcoholic overdose,' he murmured. 'Better get some black coffee into them.'

The paramedic pushing the trolley shrugged his shoulders. 'I think they've been drinking all the way from Calais,' he said. 'They were fiddling with the door mechanism of the bus. When the driver turned into a service station to try and calm them down, the door opened and about six of them fell out and rolled down an embankment into a field.'

Tania wrinkled her nose. 'They smell as if they've rolled into a load of manure,' she said. 'Looks like the first treatment should be a good hose-down!'

Connie turned to Emma. 'Would you and Tania deal with this stretchered patient, please? Take him to the small theatre and do the usual obs—find out why he's in such pain. Try and ignore the flood from the ceiling in the corner! The rest of you, clean up the walking wounded and look them over—they may need X-rays. Remember, alcohol can mask a few conditions very well.'

It didn't take long to get back into the swing of things, reflected Emma as the team clicked into a well-established routine. It had been two months since she'd left her last job, but there was a familiarity in the practice of examining any patient that didn't change just because it was a different hospital. She smiled reassuringly at Bert Foley, and rubbed her hands together to warm them before gently feeling the man's ribcage to establish if there was any misalignment.

He was obviously in great pain, giving sharp gasps of discomfort, stiffening his body even before Emma had touched him, his eyes wide with apprehension.

'Don't worry—I know you're in pain, but we can do something about that. I'm just checking where the areas of particular tenderness are—I think you've bruised your chest—and the cure for that is going to be lots of rest. Try and relax whilst Sister Cornish swabs those cuts for you on your face and arms.'

Tania was cleaning the wounds and picking out debris with small forceps, having cut away his clothes. The man grunted and said thickly, 'I don't normally have attention like this from two good-looking women!'

Tania winked at Emma. 'You men—you'll do anything to get attention!' she teased.

Emma smiled. She had a feeling she and Tania were going to get on well, and it was a good sign when the patient made some response. She looked up as Connie came into the room. The registrar was accompanied by someone else, and at first Emma paid no attention to the tall man at Connie's side.

'How's Mr Foley?' Connie enquired quietly at the side of the patient. 'Any idea what's causing the pain?'

'Tentative diagnosis of chest bruising. But he's alert and there's no sign of shock—his BP and pulse are OK. I guess he had a sharp blow to his chest when he fell out of the bus.'

Connie nodded. 'That's fairly common in impact accidents.' She turned to the man by her side. 'What do you think, Sean?'

'He may have cracked ribs—he'll need plenty of analgesia for the pain and breathing exercises to keep his lungs clear. We'll do an X-ray to be on the safe side.'

The deep voice sounded rather familiar. Emma looked up at the speaker with a moment's astonishment, then she swallowed hard in disbelief as she recognised him—the aquiline nose, deep-set blue eyes. They could only belong to her companion in the taxi! Was there a horrible chance that this man actually *worked* in this department? How ironic was that!

'We're going to keep you in for the night,' Connie was explaining to Mr Foley. 'You'll be given an injection for the pain and we want to monitor your respiration for twenty-four hours. I've already rung Medical and luckily there is a bed available.'

Bert looked mournfully at Emma. 'Don't know what my wife's going to say,' he muttered. 'I'm supposed to be looking after the kids for two nights while she goes off with her girl friends to London. That's why she let me go to the football match. That's the last time I'll be allowed to do that!'

He gazed gloomily in front of him as he was wheeled away to X-Ray.

'Well, well, so *you're* the new registrar! Fancy our paths crossing again so soon.' Connie's companion stepped forward and stood in front of Emma, looking down at her with a quizzical expression.

Emma surveyed his tall figure and the austere, good-looking face with resignation. 'Yes, indeed…fancy,' she replied in a hollow voice.

'I didn't realise when we met that you were coming to work here. That's quite a coincidence.'

Connie looked at them both with a bright, surprised smile. 'So, Emma, you've met Sean Casey, our specialist registrar, already? No need for introductions, then…' She turned to Sean. 'The poor girl had a terrible time getting here apparently. Not only were the trains on a go-slow but she had to fight with some obnoxious man to get a taxi.'

One corner of Sean's mouth twitched and he folded his arms in front of him.

'Did she really? I imagine that it was on a par with my struggle to get here on time as well…' Then he stepped forward and held out his hand, saying gravely, 'I'm glad you managed to make it in spite of your difficulties, Emma. I hope you'll be very happy here.'

Emma cleared her throat and said with an attempt at brightness, 'I'm sure I will be.'

Connie had left the small theatre, and Sean and Emma were alone. Emma felt a mixture of annoyance and apprehension. This man had demonstrated his ability to be one of the rudest and most arrogant men she'd met in a long while, and it was, she thought ruefully, Sod's law that she had to end up working with him!

She flicked a look at the confident, self-assured face, obviously used to getting his own way, and mentally shrugged her shoulders. She wasn't going to be cowed by the man—she needed the work and she'd just have to make the best of the situation.

'We didn't get round to exchanging names when we met. What's your surname?' he enquired.

'It's Fulford—Emma Fulford.'

A second's silence, then he remarked casually, 'Any relation to Professor Fulford, the cardiologist?'

Emma bit her lip—she'd rather her connections had been kept anonymous but, short of changing her name, that was difficult to do. 'Yes,' she admitted, 'he was my father.'

'Your father? Ah...I see.'

His attitude seemed to change suddenly, and there was a sharpness in his voice that made Emma look at him curiously. What does he see? she wondered. Does he think I've got the job because of my father? Sean's expression was unreadable, but it was just the type of thing someone like him *would* think!

'I had an interview, like everyone else,' she said defensively. 'I don't expect any favours.'

He smiled, but it was a frosty smile that didn't reach his eyes. 'Of course not—your father certainly wouldn't have countenanced that. He was a man who expected everyone to make their own way in life, to seize any opportunities that presented themselves.'

Sean's tone suggested that he didn't admire this ideal, as if he thought it a selfish attitude towards life. He didn't like my father, thought Emma with sudden perception. She lifted her chin with a defiant air.

'My father was all for me being independent. He encouraged me in my career—he never spoonfed me.'

Sean bowed his head slightly as if acknowledging her words. 'And where have you been working up till now?'

'At St Augustine's down South—a large inner-city hospital. I've come back to Carrfield to support my mother now she's widowed. She lives a little way out of town, but I shall come in by car in future as the trains are so unreliable.'

And why am I telling him all this? Emma wondered irritably. He didn't need to know her personal details. After all, she wasn't working here for good—she was just a short-term locum. The less she told Sean Casey about her personal affairs, the better.

'Provided you can find a parking space in this hospital, it would certainly be easier for you to get to work by car,' Sean remarked, then, as if he was making an effort to be pleasant, he gave a ghost of a smile. 'Then you wouldn't have to fight obnoxious men for a taxi from the station, would you?'

Emma gave an unwilling chuckle. Perhaps Sean did have a certain charm when he wanted to exert it—but she wasn't going to be won over all that easily. Her experience with her father had taught her that bullies could be quite engaging when they weren't being opposed—she'd already seen how this man could react when he didn't get what he wanted!

'Hopefully,' she said pertly, 'the situation over taxis won't arise again.'

There was a sudden hiatus behind her and Katie, the receptionist, appeared in the doorway, twisting her hands together nervously.

'Something the matter, Katie?' asked Sean.

'In the waiting room...' said Katie hesitantly. 'Everyone's busy with the bus victims, and this old man's come in—and he's just *gushing* blood,' she added dramatically. 'It looks terrible, there's blood everywhere...'

'Get Zak to stir himself and bring a wheelchair,' Sean said brusquely, referring to a young porter leaning nonchalantly against a wall in the corridor and chewing gum. His voice had the terse authority of someone used to giving orders. 'And tell him to stop chewing that disgusting stuff when he's on duty.'

They walked briskly to Reception—Katie's vivid description of the scene hadn't been too far off the mark. An elderly couple were sitting together near the door, the wife trying ineffectually to staunch the flow of blood from her husband's nose with a handkerchief.

'He's called Mr Anstruther—Percy Anstruther,' said Katie as Sean strode quickly over to the two anxious old people and squatted by the man, putting a reassuring hand on his arm.

'Don't worry, Mr Anstruther,' he said comfortingly. 'We'll take you through to a cubicle now and try and stop that bleed for you. We have some tricks up our sleeve that should help.'

The old man nodded and his wife turned a frightened face to Sean. 'He's lost so much blood, Doctor,' she said in a quavery voice. 'Will he need a blood transfusion?'

'Hopefully not—nosebleeds often look worse than they are. But we'll do some tests on your husband and see if we can establish why it started in the first place.'

Sean's voice was gentle and kindly, quite different

in manner to his curt tone in the taxi, Emma reflected in some surprise. Mr Anstruther had relaxed enough to manage a weak smile.

'It's good blood I'm losing here,' he mumbled. 'You'll find it's 80 per cent proof!'

The old gentleman was transferred to a cubicle bed, and Tania adjusted the bed and pillow so that he was propped in a semi-upright position.

'How old is Mr Anstruther?' Emma asked his wife.

'We're both eighty-seven.' She looked in bewilderment at Emma. 'He's never had anything like this before—it happened so sudden, like. One minute he was reading the paper and the next he was pouring blood!'

'BP's a bit high,' murmured Sean, as he unwound the cuff of the sphygmomanometer he'd been using. 'Is your husband on blood-pressure tablets Mrs Anstruther?'

'Yes, he was, but he's run out of them. Our son usually gets his prescription, but he hasn't been for a while…'

The old lady stopped for a second and dabbed at her eyes, looking very distressed.

'Not to worry—first thing is to stop the bleed. We're going to pack your nose with gauze, Mr Anstruther. It won't be very comfortable, but hopefully it will do the trick.' Sean turned to Emma. 'It would be a good idea to take some bloods and find out what his haemoglobin's like.'

As Emma took some blood from the old man she said casually, 'What about us getting in touch with your son? I'm sure he'd want to know that his father's ill.'

The elderly couple looked at each other for a second and Emma saw the flash of apprehension in their eyes.

Mrs Anstruther quavered, ‘Oh, no—that wouldn’t do at all, would it, Percy? Ron wouldn’t want to come—that is, he’s very busy, you know, and it would take him nearly an hour to get here. We don’t want to worry him. You just get Percy’s nose right, and we’ll be on our way quite happily.’

‘You know, most chemists will deliver your prescriptions these days,’ suggested Emma, labelling the phial of blood to be sent off for analysis. ‘You might find that easier than relying on your son coming over. Have you any other children?’

The old lady shook her head. ‘Only Ron…he’s married with a young family. Of course they’re all very busy….’ Her voice tailed off wistfully.

Emma began to get the feeling that their son wasn’t too interested in what happened to his parents, and she felt a sudden rush of pity for the frail couple, almost, it seemed to her, frightened of their only child.

Half an hour later both doctors came back to the cubicle and Sean examined the packed gauze in Mr Anstruther’s nose. Blood still flowed out of the nostril when he disturbed the packing.

‘It doesn’t seem to be doing much good, does it?’ said Emma. ‘Do you think we should cauterise the vein?’

‘I think you’re right,’ he agreed. He smiled down at the old man. ‘You’re determined to keep us on our toes, aren’t you, sir? We’ll do as my colleague suggests.’ He turned to Emma. ‘I think we’ll give our patient some Haemaccel as well. He’s looking a bit white—he must have had quite a bit of fluid loss.’

Emma nodded. 'I'll get Tania to set up a drip. Have Mr Anstruther's blood results come back yet?'

Sean glanced at a piece of paper in his hand. 'Yes—his blood count is rather low. I think we should keep you in for the night, Mr Anstruther.'

'But what good would that do?' asked his wife.

'It may well have picked up by tomorrow morning—but if it hasn't we'd like to do some further investigations as to why he's anaemic. And, of course, he's still bleeding—we must get that under control.'

The couple looked at each other in consternation and Emma said gently. 'Are you going to be all right getting home on your own, Mrs Anstruther?'

Just as the old lady was about to reply, Katie appeared. 'There's a gentleman here to see Mr Anstruther,' she announced. 'It's his son.'

'Ah.' Sean smiled, 'That's lucky—he's come at the right time! Perhaps he'll be able to take you home, Mrs Anstruther, so that you can get a good rest.'

The Anstruthers didn't reply, but seemed worried as they looked at the small bald-headed man who'd appeared through the curtain. The young Mr Anstruther barely glanced at the doctors in the cubicle, but looked at his parents accusingly.

'Well, I must say, you've led me a dance!' His voice was plaintive, as if he'd been very put out. 'I was in a meeting when your neighbour rang to say she'd seen an ambulance come to the house. You might have told me yourselves, then I wouldn't have had to disrupt everything to come over just for a nosebleed!'

There was a shocked silence, then Mrs Anstruther said shakily, 'We didn't want to bother you, dear. Like you, we thought a nosebleed couldn't do much harm, but it just seemed to go on and on...'

Sean stepped forward and said smoothly but with a distinctly curt edge to his voice, 'This isn't quite as minor a problem as you suggest, Mr Anstruther. Your father is having a very bad bleed. As you can appreciate, at his age this isn't a minor matter and he's in some shock.'

Emma smiled to herself. Sean certainly knew how to assert his authority in a quiet but firm manner. The old man's son looked slightly abashed.

'So what's going to happen?'

'We'll keep your father in, certainly for at least one night. Until we're sure we've stopped the bleed and his haemoglobin's at an acceptable level, we want to monitor him. However, when you're ready, you can take your mother home.'

Ronald sighed heavily. 'I don't know if she'll be all right on her own,' he said, as if his mother wasn't present. 'They really should be in a home somewhere—I'm always telling them that. I haven't the time to keep coming over whenever there's a crisis. If they sold off their great big house there'd be plenty of money, and at least someone could keep an eye on them.'

His mother dabbed her eyes, suppressing a half-sob, and Sean's lips tightened ominously.

'I really think that your parents' future plans should be discussed when they're more able to cope—certainly not at the moment. Right now they need all the support they can get.'

Ron Anstruther sighed heavily. 'Oh, well, I'm just

thinking of them. I suppose you'd better come and stay with us,' he said ungraciously to his mother.

Mrs Anstruther got up from her chair rather unsteadily, but her voice was suddenly firm and dignified. 'No, Ron. You don't need to worry—I'm certainly not going to inconvenience you and Kath. I shall go home by taxi when I've seen your father safely to the ward. I prefer my own bed anyway. You get back to your meeting. We'll be quite all right.'

An expression of shocked surprise crossed Ron's face. 'I didn't mean we didn't want you,' he said with an attempt at grace.

'Please, go now,' said his mother. 'I don't care what you say, but we want to be alone and I definitely do *not* want a lift from you.'

Her son's face reddened. 'I only came to help,' he muttered, 'But you can't help some people, can you?' He looked at Sean and Emma defensively. 'Parents, eh?'

Then he turned abruptly and went out of the cubicle. Mrs Anstruther sat down on the chair again and gave a shaky laugh.

'He doesn't mean to be insensitive,' she said sadly. 'It's because he's an only child, I think. He feels the responsibility of us on his shoulders—and, I have to say, his wife is a very difficult woman!'

Two wheelchairs were found for the Anstruthers and they were taken to the medical ward so that Mr Anstruther could be admitted. Sean watched them go rather grimly.

'What have that lovely old couple done to deserve that terrible son?' he said. 'Just wait till he's old and ill...'

Emma looked at him quickly. Sean Casey, she decided, had more facets to his character than she'd imagined, and despite herself she warmed to the compassion in Sean's voice.

'You managed to keep your cool with him,' she observed. 'I think I might have said something very unprofessional to that creep!'

He looked at her quizzically. 'That I can believe! I'm sure you could say something fairly cutting to young Mr Anstruther—and he'd deserve it too!'

He shot a look at his watch and went into the central area beyond the cubicles where the computers held updates on admissions and punched a few keys.

'Nice and quiet at the moment,' he said, squinting at the screen. 'I don't know about you, Dr Fulford, but I could do with a cup of strong black coffee after that little episode!'

The last thing she'd expected to be doing when she'd arrived at Casualty that morning, reflected Emma, was to be drinking coffee with Sean Casey an hour later, let alone be working with him in the same department! She looked at him under her lashes as he peered at a work sheet on the wall of the staffroom. One had to admit the man had presence—tall, well built, with a thick crop of black hair which stood up rather spikily round his head. But looks could be very deceiving, she reminded herself. A man who could be as rude as he had been to her earlier in the day obviously had a temper—she wondered how often his colleagues had witnessed it.

He turned round to her as if aware of her curious eyes boring into his back.

'So what made you leave Carrfield before for St Augustine's?' he asked, putting a heaped teaspoon of sugar into his coffee.

She paused for a second, slightly unprepared for that question and the painful memories it brought back. Funny how the thought of those memories were so vivid even after three years, and how it still brought an ache to her heart.

Then she replied lightly, 'I wanted to spread my wings. I…I thought it would give me some good experience to move away for a while—have my own space.'

He nodded. Was there a hint of a sigh in his reply? 'I can imagine that.'

'You've always worked round here?'

'Except for a year as a junior doctor in the teaching hospital after med school. I decided to come back to Carrfeld when my family circumstances changed. But I love it around here—the countryside, the sea. This hospital must have one of the most wonderful views in England.'

Emma wondered what the changes in his family circumstances had been—marriage, children? She could imagine that a confident man like him would have a perfect background—a beautiful wife and two lovely children—and probably rule the roost like her father had in their family!

She sipped her coffee then said boldly, 'And is your wife from a medical background?'

He looked at her with amusement. 'What made you think I was married?'

Emma bit her lip, slightly embarrassed by her curiosity. 'I'm sorry—I just assumed when you mentioned ''family circumstances'' that you had a family.'

'A pleasure yet to come,' Sean said drily. His mouth tightened, a troubled expression appeared on his face. 'I have other matters that take up my time at the moment,' he said briefly.

His blue eyes looked at her stonily as if daring her to pursue the matter. Sean was not going to elaborate on his private life, but somehow he had revealed a chink in his armour, a slight vulnerability that was not unattractive.

There was a short silence between them, then he said smoothly, turning the conversation adroitly back to Emma, 'So now you've come back to support your mother. She's lucky that you can do that.'

'It's something I wanted to do—and I think in my circumstances it could work out well.'

He gazed at her thoughtfully. 'Do you have a family yourself—children?'

Emma took a deep sip of coffee. 'No—I'm not married and I don't have a partner now.'

Her tone was light, inconsequential, giving nothing away. Sean's glance flicked over her astutely—perhaps he sensed that her easy manner hid deeper emotions.

'I'm surprised…a pretty girl like you…'

Emma looked scornfully at him—how arrogant and patronising could you get? Did he think she'd be flattered by such a trite remark? It was almost a disappointment that someone with Sean Casey's intelligence would come out with the same old flattering mush—and there was no way she was going to be taken in by that! Hadn't she learned a long time ago that honeyed words did not necessarily spell sincerity?

Sean watched her expression and put down his mug, looking slightly rueful. 'Put my foot in it, have I? I didn't mean to be banal.'

Emma was silent, cross with herself for showing her feelings. After all, she had to work with this man, didn't she? No good making an enemy out of him.

He looked at her warily over his mug. 'It *was* meant to be a compliment. Rather a corny thing to say perhaps...but true.'

She made an effort to be gracious. 'Then thank you. I'm afraid I do tend to show my feelings too much—my father told me that often enough!'

'You remind me very much of your father in certain ways.'

'In what way? Not his more difficult traits, I hope?'

'No,' he replied with surprising emphasis. 'I'm thinking of his competence—you've shown that this morning. And you're forthright, like he was!'

'You knew him well, then?'

Sean's expression hardened. 'Well enough. We came across each other at work, of course, and I was on a committee with him.'

Emma looked at him perceptively. 'But you didn't get on with him, did you?'

Sean was silent for a second, then, as if he was unwilling to say more, he remarked tersely, 'He could be damn difficult—but he was thorough. I was glad I didn't actually work in his department—we would not have made good colleagues.' He looked at her wryly. 'I never thought I would be working with his daughter.'

She looked at Sean candidly. 'I know my father wasn't the easiest of men, but I imagine you were able to stand up to him.'

Sean shrugged. 'I was rather a junior doctor—your father was eminent in his field. He could be quite crushing and, of course, he was very influential—people took notice of him.'

It was intriguing—something had occurred between Professor Fulford and Sean Casey, and the younger doctor obviously still held a grudge even after her father's death.

'Then I will try not to be as difficult as he was,' Emma said crisply.

He gave the sudden unexpected smile that seemed to change his face to a softer, gentler character. 'I have a feeling that we can overcome any problems we might encounter, and I look forward to a good working relationship from now on—don't you?'

It felt as if Sean was offering her an olive branch. His wrist brushed against hers momentarily, and she looked up to see a hint of apology in his blue gaze. Emma stared back at him and that extraordinary feeling of excitement edged with danger which had come over her once before that morning surged through her like the crackle of an electric current, and a longing for something she'd not had for many years rippled through her with peculiar intensity.

'Yes,' she said slightly breathlessly. 'Yes, I'm sure we can work well together.'

She rinsed her mug under the tap vigorously, hoping he hadn't noticed her flustered response, but he merely nodded briskly and walked off to answer a phone.

Emma's eyes followed him as he disappeared round the corner, the thoughts in her head whirling round like ingredients in a mixer. What the hell was happening to her? She didn't like Sean Casey's type—she hadn't *wanted* to like the man at all from the moment she'd met him. He'd obviously disliked her father for some reason, and probably resented her presence, so surely what she felt wasn't attraction? Why, then, was she reacting to him as if he'd just pressed every erogenous zone in her body?

She bit her lip. It had been over three years since she'd reacted in this way to a man—three years since she'd vowed never to be attracted in that way again. Just because a good-looking man smiled at her, she seemed to have forgotten any lessons she had learned so harshly in the past.

'You all right, Emma?' Tania's voice broke into her thoughts as she bustled into the room. 'Think you're going to enjoy working with our Superdoc?'

'Er...Superdoc?'

Tania laughed. 'Why, the delectable Sean Casey, of course—he's sent quite a few blood pressures soaring, I can tell you.'

Emma hoped the blush she felt rising up her face was not too obvious. 'I don't like mixing business with pleasure,' she said primly. 'Anyway, I've a strong feeling he's got a fiery temper.'

'You can say that again.' Tania sighed theatrically. 'I wouldn't care about that—if I wasn't a happily married woman I'd risk his temper!'

'I think,' said Emma carefully, 'I'm going to be far too busy to get interested in someone like Dr Casey!'

'Huh!' remarked Tania, lifting a large box of sterile dressings out of a cupboard. 'Don't you be too sure, my girl—not many of us are immune to his charms!'

Then I'll be one of the few, thought Emma. She wasn't in the market for romance after her previous experience of falling hook, line and sinker for a gorgeous-looking man had all ended in tears.

CHAPTER TWO

EMMA had always loved the house. Even when her father had been alive and ruling the household with a rod of iron, and the atmosphere had sometimes been strained and frightening, she had found comfort in the gracious splendour of its rooms. Professor Fulford had loved the house too, pouring money into reconstructing the older part, adding a beautiful conservatory. Perched on the cliff a few miles down the coast from the hospital, it commanded a wonderful view, with spacious rooms looking over rolling lawns. Beyond the sloping lawn was the sea, glinting in the sun sometimes or lashing itself into a white fury against the cliffs. There was always a different mood to look at. Now she wondered sadly how long it would be before her mother put the place on the market. It was far too big for one person, and although Emma was staying there at the moment, she intended to get her own place soon. Charles, her brother, had left home when he'd got married and now lived about an hour's drive away.

'So how did your first day go back at the hospital?' Mrs Fulford's neat little figure was perched on the sofa as she sipped a drink and looking fondly at her daughter.

'It was good—most of them seem really nice.' Emma paused, and examined her nails rather intently, then said casually, 'Have you ever met a man called Sean Casey? He's the specialist registrar. He said he knew Dad—they were on the same committee together.'

Mrs Fulford stared at her daughter strangely for a second, then got up abruptly and walked over to the window, her voice rather strained. 'I do remember him quite well—rather a striking-looking young man—but I don't think your father took to him much.' She gave a short brittle laugh and turned round to Emma, her eyes a little bright. 'But, then, Robert didn't like anyone who stood up to him! I seem to recall this Dr Casey telling your father that it was out of order for his department to get all the money that had been left to the hospital in some legacy. Nobody else dared say that, and I don't think Robert ever forgave him!'

'So did Dad give way?' asked Emma, intrigued by the story and wishing she'd witnessed the scene when Sean and her father had clashed!

'As I remember, he was forced for once in his life to capitulate—but Sean Casey was enemy number one as far as Robert was concerned after that.' Emma was surprised at the bitter tone in her mother's voice. 'They certainly didn't like each other.'

Emma had detected over the last few weeks a new resolution in her mother's attitude—a gradual emerging of a more robust character, battered by many years of bullying. For Mrs Fulford to criticise her husband when he'd been alive would have been unthinkable, although thought Emma drily to herself she had had plenty of reason to. Now, it seemed, she was prepared to look at him more objectively.

'I can imagine they could have had some pretty sparky encounters. I had a spat myself with Sean Casey in the taxi going to the hospital before I knew I was working with him—he was extremely rude!'

'Not a good start, then? Thinks he rules the place, does he?' Her mother smiled faintly, then she added with more force, 'Some of these men get too big for their boots, I think. Don't let him bully you, Emma—keep away from men like that.'

'I guess he's good at his job,' conceded Emma. She thought of the gentle way he'd handled the Anstruthers and kept their son in check—he'd been quite impressive then. 'But I can imagine he'd stand up for himself if crossed. Anyway I'm sure we'll manage to get along OK—after all, I'm not there for ever. I'm not going to let someone like him worry me.'

Even as she spoke, her heart quickened. The fact was that since her encounter with him over coffee, it had been hard to stop thinking about the man and her extraordinary reaction to him.

Her mother sighed. 'You shouldn't have given up your job and come back here when your father died—you were doing so well. After all, Charles is only an hour away and he'd come over if I needed him.'

Emma raised her eyebrows—she'd never been convinced of her brother's reliability. 'He's got other things on his mind, hasn't he? He's got a three-year-old to look after, which means he hasn't much time for anything else.' She paused and smiled fondly at her mother. 'Anyway, you know I wanted to come back, Mum. I love it round here, always have, and although it will be a blow to sell this place, we'll have fun looking for somewhere else for you.'

Mrs Fulford gazed out at the warm evening sun that

had replaced the rain earlier in the day, her hands twisting nervously together.

'I've been thinking about that, Emma,' she said slowly, turning to face her daughter. 'And you may think I'm completely impractical—but I don't want to sell Cliff House.'

'But it's so big for one person. And I hate to mention it, but the place needs a lot of upkeep.'

'You're right, of course.' Her mother paused, then looked with barely suppressed excitement at her daughter. 'Don't think I'm mad—but I've been pondering an idea I've had. Why don't I turn it into a superior sort of bed and breakfast? I've always thought it would lend itself to that—and, of course, before I was married I was in catering. Don't you think it could be fun?'

Emma stared at her mother in amazement. 'What?' she said stupidly. '*You* run a B and B?' Then, realising that she sounded rather insulting, she added quickly, 'Not that I think you couldn't do it—you're a wonderful cook and it's a great house for it.'

'You see,' her mother went on eagerly, 'I'm not completely decrepit. I want to do something now I'm on my own, and I'm sure there's a market for it. We get so many tourists in the summer I feel we could fill this place easily.'

Mrs Fulford's pretty little face was flushed with enthusiasm and Emma realised that this was her mother's leap to independence. After years of trotting in the wake of her husband, now she could be in charge of her own life—do something she wanted to do.

Emma walked over to her mother and hugged her. 'I think it could be a wonderful idea,' she said. 'Have you been planning it for a while?'

Her mother nodded. 'I've always had a yearning to be my own boss—and there is another consideration. Now Charles is on his own and has little Ben to look after, he could come here and help with the books and so on, do the heavy work. It would be lovely for Ben to grow up in this place.'

Emma nodded doubtfully. Her brother had never really found his niche at work, trying out various schemes to little effect but never really sticking at anything, and he and she did not really get on.

'It would be lovely for Ben. Since Annette left Charles I think the little boy needs some stability in his life.'

'I've mentioned it to Charles, and he sounds very enthusiastic,' said Mrs Fulford. 'Do you think it could work out?'

'I think it sounds very exciting—I just hope he is the right person to help you.' Emma grinned at her mother. 'But don't take any notice of my quibbles. Anyway, if you aren't going to be looking for a new home, I think I shall have to find somewhere to live nearer the hospital anyway.'

She looked out of the window. 'It's so lovely now I might just go and stretch my legs along the shore and have a squint at the estate agents' windows nearer Carrfield.'

'You do that—you need some fresh air after your first day in the hospital. I'll have a good meal waiting for you when you get back.'

'I'm going to miss your wonderful cooking when I move.' Emma smiled.

She went upstairs and quickly changed from her navy trouser suit into a pair of cropped jeans and a white shirt—after the rain and storm of the morning, it had turned into a balmy early summer evening.

Emma opened the gate at the bottom of the garden and ran down the little rocky path that led to the beach. Buttery yellow clusters of primroses still nestled on the grassy bank and there was the odd flash of blue as cornflowers started to open up in the more sheltered places. Gradually her mood began to lift from the irritation of the morning's early events and the stress of her first day at a new job. It was so wonderful to be back in the place she loved best in the world—such a contrast to the inner-city hospital she'd just left, where going for a walk in the evening meant strolling through heavily built-up areas before one came to any open spaces.

She drew a deep breath of satisfaction, smelling the tangy scent of the sea, feeling the oxygen hit her lungs like a draught of wine, the sun warm on her arms. She watched a small motor boat buzz across the bay, pulling a waterskier behind it, the evening sun making the wake sparkle. After the traumas three years ago when she'd left Carrfield, it was doubly wonderful to be back. And now she had the excitement of looking for a place of her own to live in, and the added satisfaction that her mother seemed to have plans for the future.

She reached the beach and her feet made a crunching sound on the shingle as she walked briskly along the shoreline. Her thoughts drifted back to her day at the hospital, and to her irritation a narrow face with strong features and incredible eyes floated into her mind. Despite the fact that Sean Casey had got under her skin as soon as she'd met him, she was shaken by her unexpected response to the man—and intrigued by the disagreement between her father and him. She wondered if it would colour Sean's attitude towards her. She shrugged. There must have been many people who'd come up against Professor Fulford, but nevertheless her father had put Carrfield on the map with his innovative procedures and many patients would be everlastingly grateful to him.

The beach seemed deserted. Far away in the distance Emma could see a man out for an evening run with a dog lolloping beside him. Nearer at hand the motor boat had swung in towards the shore so that it could cast off its waterskier near a little rocky inlet and onto the soft sand. It seemed to be coming in quite fast—Emma watched it in the evening sun. The waterskier was still doing impressive turns on one ski, but as the boat turned parallel to the shore Emma heard the driver shout something at the skier. It was then she realised to her horror that the boat's circle had taken it perilously near to the rocks and that the skier was heading very fast towards them.

She stood still, paralysed by inaction, watched the skier drop the tow rope and desperately try to zigzag away from the danger. Then there was a horrible scraping noise as the ski bounced and scored its way over the rocks, until the skier lost his balance and fell over, his body ricocheting sickeningly from boulder to boulder, and she heard him give a thin high scream.

'My God,' whispered Emma, her mouth dry.

She started to run towards the stricken man, clambering over rocks made slippery by seaweed and water, oblivious to the scratches on her hands and legs. She watched in horror as his inert body slithered down a rock and back into the sea.

'I'm coming!' she called. 'Hang on in there, I'll be with you in a moment!'

The young man was floating in the water, a stain of blood spreading from his legs and stomach into the sea like ink on a blotter. Emma tore off her jeans and slipped into the water, gasping as the cold hit her. The man was being carried out by a slight current but she reached him without too much difficulty and grabbed hold of his life jacket. His eyes were closed and he looked desperately pale.

'Here I am,' she yelled as loudly as she could, trying to rouse him. His eyelids fluttered and she breathed a sigh of relief. At least he was alive! She started to tow him slowly and painfully round the rocks and towards the little spit of sand which he'd been trying to aim for. It was exhausting. His body bobbed up and down and he was quite a large man. Emma gasped as she used every ounce of energy to try and push him in front of her, salt water filling her mouth and nose.

Every time she made a little headway, the undertow would pull her back again, and she was beginning to wonder if she'd ever make it. She closed her eyes with the effort.

'It's all right...you can let go. I've got him, don't worry. Just concentrate on getting yourself back.'

The weight of the victim she was pushing suddenly lessened, and the voice beside her was loud and commanding. Emma opened her eyes in amazed relief—thankfully someone had come to help. She felt she could not have gone on for very much longer. She trod water to get her strength back for a minute and through blurred eyes watched the young man being pulled strongly to the shore by a powerful-looking figure. In the background a dog was barking frantically. Never had she felt more grateful or relieved that help had been at hand. With renewed strength she swam back to the beach and staggered out of the water as the rescuer pulled the victim onto the sand.

'Thank you, thank you,' she gasped. 'If you hadn't come along, I don't think I'd ever have got him in.'

'You did damn well—he's a big lad. He's lucky you were around.'

The man had his ear to the youth's chest, listening to his breathing. He turned round to look at Emma and his eyes widened. They were very blue eyes—eyes she'd been thinking of only ten minutes before.

'Good heavens,' said Sean. 'Not you again!'

Emma gaped at him with equal astonishment. 'How extraordinary. What are you doing here?'

'I live near here,' said Sean briefly. 'I was doing my evening run when I saw this guy scrape over the rocks and you go in after him. We'd better get some help—he's bleeding badly, probably concussed. Stay with him, will you? My cottage is up on the cliffs there. I haven't got my mobile with me so I'll run up and phone from there.' He turned to a black Labrador standing by him, whining with excitement. 'Quiet, Rocket—we're going back.'

Sean and the dog ran up the slope, then the sound of the motor boat's engine coming towards them made Emma turn round. The engine cut out and the driver leapt out of the boat and splashed towards them. He looked wild with worry, his voice strained and hoarse.

'Is he all right? I tried to warn him…I shouted that there were rocks in the way, but I was too late.'

He knelt over the prone figure of the victim.

'Neil…Neil, oh, God, I'm sorry.' He looked frantically across at Emma. 'We've got to get help—he looks terrible.' He put his head in his hands and said in a muffled, cracked voice, 'It's all my fault. I took the corner too sharply.'

Emma spoke calmly, trying to encourage the distraught man to take a cue from her and keep in control. 'Don't worry—the man who pulled him in has run up to his cottage to phone for an ambulance. In the meantime, have you got a rug in your boat, or a pullover—something we could cover him with?'

Glad to have something to do, the young man raced back to the boat, hauling it further onto the sand, and took a woollen blanket from one of the seats. Emma gently placed the blanket over Neil's battered body.

'Take off your T-shirt,' she said to Neil's friend. 'It looks relatively clean and I can use it as a pad to try and stop the bleeding to his head. What's your name?'

'Gerry—I'm Neil's cousin. He was practising for a competition to be held here this weekend… Oh, God, what have I done?' He tore off his T-shirt and handed it to Emma.

Sean ran down the cliffside with yet more blankets and some teatowels. 'These towels are clean and have no fluff on them—perhaps we could put them over the bleed on the chest area,' he suggested. He looked down at Neil with an assessing frown. 'I've a suspicion about his right leg—looks out of alignment to me.'

'What do you mean?' asked his cousin anxiously.

'I think it's probably broken. What do you think, Emma? Fracture of fibula?'

A faint sound of an ambulance siren floated over to them, getting louder every second.

'That was a fast response,' said Sean. 'I also rang Casualty to tell them what was coming. Connie's still on duty and she's well prepared.'

Gerry looked at him in puzzlement. 'You seem to know what to do—are you a medical man?'

Sean smiled faintly as he felt the victim's pulse. 'Both of us are. We've just finished for the day—or thought we had!' He turned to Emma and said in a low voice, 'Pulse thready, breathing shallow, could be internal bleeding, possibly his spleen.'

'Is that why Neil's so pale? Is it because he's bleeding?' Gerry's voice was querulous, overwrought.

Emma leant back on her heels. 'Neil's in shock—that is, he's had a dangerous reduction of blood flow throughout his body tissues. I'd like to raise his legs and try and to get the blood flowing to his upper body but I'm mindful he could have a back injury. They'll pick that up in Casualty. Until we know the extent of his injuries, it's better not to move him too much.'

The ambulance was now parked at the top of the cliff, a curious crowd of onlookers gathered round it, watching as the paramedics ran down towards the victim, carrying a stretcher and medical bags. Behind them followed two policemen at a slower pace.

'I thought you'd finished duty today, Doctor,' said one of the paramedics. 'Can't keep you away, eh?'

'Hello, Brian,' said Sean. He drew him to one side, away from Neil. 'This young man is eighteen, his name's Neil and he's been waterskiing over the rocks. He's got a query fractured fibula, possible internal bleeding from somewhere—could be spleen.'

Brian gave a low whistle. 'Pity he didn't stick to the water,' he murmured, before going over to Neil. He took a small instrument out of his pack and placed a peg from it on the victim's finger. 'This little beauty should tell us what his BP is and blood oxygen sats are…' He looked at the gauge and pulled down his mouth. 'Not too good, eighty over fifty.'

'That's an oximeter,' explained Sean to Gerry, who was watching everything with mounting anxiety. 'It can tell us all kinds of things about the state of the patient—how much oxygen is getting to his blood, his breathing rate, blood pressure…'

Brian and his colleague were working hard, slipping a collar round Neil's neck, then strapping him to a board to keep his spine supported and straight. Finally they lifted him carefully onto a carrying stretcher and started to walk slowly up the path to the ambulance.

'It might be a good idea to give him some Haemaccel on the way,' suggested Sean. 'I should think he's suffering from fluid loss.'

'Aye, aye, Doc,' said Brian. 'We'll give him some oxygen as well. See you later.'

Emma turned to the stricken-looking Gerry. 'Why don't you go with him? Then you can ring his parents or whoever when you know what's happening.'

'Of course, you're right, I've got to be with him—he'll need someone, won't he?'

'Well, then,' said one of the policemen, 'we'll come back with you to the hospital and take a statement. Are you a relative?'

'I'm his cousin,' said Gerry dolefully.

The young man followed the paramedics dejectedly up the cliff, turning after a few steps. 'Thank you…thanks, both of you. You saved him. I don't know what would have happened if you hadn't been there.'

The two doctors watched the little cavalcade make its way up to the ambulance, then Sean turned to Emma, his expression concerned. He took one of the towels he'd brought down with him and pulled it round her.

'You must be feeling exhausted and freezing. I don't know how you managed to bring that boy in so close to the shore. He was a quite a weight.'

'I don't know either,' admitted Emma with a shaky laugh. 'If you hadn't turned up when you did, I think I might have expired as well!'

'If you hadn't been so quick off the mark, there might not have been a happy ending,' he remarked. 'Now, come back to my cottage—I've got a strong cure-all that should warm you up, and I can find something for you to put on that's better than a towel! Then I'll drive you back home—you've had enough exercise for today.'

Emma hugged the towel round her, suddenly aware that she was practically naked, her briefs and wet T-shirt not leaving much to the imagination. For the past thirty minutes there hadn't been time to consider that it was Sean she was working with, but now she was acutely conscious that it was just the two of them together. She did not want to be alone with him—she'd only known him a day, but the heady sense of dangerous excitement when he was near frightened her. She flicked a glance over his athletic figure—the khaki shorts he'd been running in revealed muscular tanned legs, his cotton top covered an impressively broad chest. She bit her lip, irritated that she should even notice his body. After all, she saw plenty of men's torsos in Casualty—albeit rather different to Sean's!

'Thanks—but it's OK,' she said in a voice that brooked no argument. 'I'm perfectly capable of getting back under my own steam.'

'Don't be ridiculous—it's getting very cool. There's a chill wind—do you want sick leave before you've even started your job properly? Look, you're shivering already!'

He took hold of her arm firmly and started to steer her up the slope of the cliff just as a man came running towards them, jacket flapping and a camera slung round his neck. He put his hand up to halt them.

'Please,' he said breathlessly. 'Can I have a word? I'm Pete Brown, a reporter on the *Carrfield Argos*—I'd really like a quick photo of you both.'

Sean frowned. 'What on earth for?'

Pete smiled engagingly at them. 'Because you're both heroes! I saw the end of the rescue of the guy in the water. It's a great story—it'll be front page news in next week's edition!'

Before either of them could say anything, he'd whipped out his camera and taken a succession of shots.

'For goodness' sake,' groaned Emma. 'I'm practically naked!'

'You look great,' enthused Pete. 'Circulation will double, I'm sure! Now, what about your names?'

'Surely we don't have to give that information?' said Sean brusquely.

The young reporter looked at them pleadingly. 'It's the first good story I've had since I've worked here—usually I'm at meetings to do with the council or the

WI. It would be nice to have my byline on a real story for once.'

Emma felt some sympathy for him—it would be a bit of a scoop for a young man just starting on his career. She looked at Sean—he looked forbidding and austere, a stubborn set about his mouth.

'I value my privacy,' he snapped. 'Just say the young man was rescued by an unknown lady.'

The reporter's face fell. 'As you like,' he said disconsolately. 'I'll go to the hospital and get the gen on the victim.' Then he grinned impishly. 'Mind you, I've got your photos, so you won't stay anonymous for long!'

For a minute Emma thought Sean's temper would get the better of him, then he shrugged resignedly. 'Ah…I forgot about that… Very well, I suppose we'll be forced to own up.'

'So…it's Mr and Mrs?' Pete asked, taking out his notebook.

'We're work colleagues,' said Emma. 'We just happened to be in the same part of the beach when the young man had his accident.'

'Pity!' remarked the reporter. 'Our readers like people to be romantically linked.'

'Sorry we can't oblige you,' said Sean drily, 'but I would be grateful if you could keep the details as simple as possible—just our names, OK? Now, could we get on with it? This lady is very chilled and needs a hot drink and warm clothes…'

A few minutes later, despite her protestations, Emma was sitting in the bright little sitting room of Sean's cottage. The evening sun was shining low through the picture window and flooding the room with a rosy light, and the sea looked as still as a millpond, belying the excitement that had occurred such a short time ago. Rocket, the dog, lay panting in a patch of sunlight under the window, watching them both with sleepy eyes.

'Quite an evening,' commented Sean as he poured her a drink. 'I suppose we can look forward to our photo plastered all over the paper tomorrow—not something I relish.'

'It'll be a nine-day wonder,' said Emma. 'People forget events very quickly—something else will happen to push it out of the headlines.'

'I hope you're right. I believe in keeping a low profile.'

Emma was vaguely surprised that a confident man like Sean should worry about appearing in the paper. What harm could it do? She sipped the hot chocolate that he had given her, the drink making a fiery path down her throat. It felt comforting and restoring. She relaxed, putting the puzzle of his dislike of any publicity to the back of her mind, and looked round in pleasure at the marvellous view.

'What a perfect spot,' she murmured. 'I should love something like this.'

'You live with your mother at the moment?'

'Yes, but I'm looking for a place of my own. My mother has just announced that she wants to turn the big family house she lives in into a bed and breakfast, so she will be busy doing that. I need my own space!'

'That's a lot for your mother to take on.'

'I think she wants to prove she can do things in her own right, have her own ideas. She was married to my father for thirty-three years.'

Sean made no comment, but raised his brows slightly as he took a swig of beer from his can.

'You think it's amazing that she could be married to him for so long?' demanded Emma, stung by his unspoken words and facial expression. 'You may not have liked him—but their marriage worked for them.'

'Then that's all that matters, isn't it?' His tone was brusque, and he turned away from her, looking out at the wonderful view for a minute. Then he moved to face her again, his voice softer, changing the subject. 'You're looking for a place in this area?'

'Yes, I need something small fairly near the hospital, and I love it around here. I haven't had a chance to look yet, though.'

Sean looked at Emma thoughtfully. 'This might not be what you want at all but there's another cottage in the little cove below—only about a hundred yards away. An old man lived there and he died a few weeks ago. I know his family want a quick sale, but it's very dilapidated and might not suit you. You can just see it from the window here.'

Emma went over to his side and he pointed down the slope of the cliff. She craned forward and saw the dark slate of the roof and the little wooden paling that fenced off a tiny garden. From what she could see it looked absolutely perfect, and she turned towards him with excitement.

'It could be just what I'm looking for!' she said eagerly. 'It must have a wonderful view, and once I'd got it straight it wouldn't need much maintenance... And I could make a lovely little rockery in front of the cottage, and—'

Sean laughed and put his hand up as if trying to slow

down her enthusiasm. 'Whoa there! I should wait until you've seen it. It may have awful drawbacks—like being too close to the sea, danger of flooding, and so on. It doesn't do to be too impulsive!'

'At least I can make enquiries, can't I? Oh, I can't wait to know all about it!'

He looked down at her eyes, sparkling up at him in pleasure, the flush of excitement in her cheeks and the russet tendrils of hair framing her face.

'I'm only saying don't get your hopes up too high,' he said gruffly after a pause 'Wealthy people tend to snap up these places as holiday cottages.'

'I shall find out tomorrow,' declared Emma. 'If I don't try, I won't get!' Unthinkingly she put her hand gratefully on his arm for a second. 'Thanks for telling me about it!'

'That's all right,' he said, smiling and holding her gaze. Then he lightly brushed away a lock of hair that was over her forehead, his fingers trailing softly over her jawline. 'It would be nice to have a sparky neighbour like you around!'

There was a short silence between them and they stared at each other, suddenly aware of their physical closeness. He was very still, watching her intently as if gauging her reaction. Then he cupped his hands gently under her chin and lifted her face to his, touching her cheek as softly as a butterfly with his mouth.

'You know, you were a heroine this afternoon. I admired you so much,' he murmured against her ear. 'I hope he realised what a lucky young man he was…'

Emma turned her head instinctively, and for a brief second their lips brushed, sending an astonishing trail of fire through her body. She tried to maintain her composure, but the atmosphere seemed charged, more intimate by the second. It was as if a small bolt of lightning had crackled through her at his touch—her lips numb where he had touched them so briefly. The crazy feeling came to her that it would be the most wonderful thing in the world if she could feel his arms around her, his body crushed against hers—and the long-forgotten sensation of desire flooded through her like a bitter-sweet memory.

She turned away abruptly, putting distance between them, frightened that he had seen how vulnerable she was to his touch, and he too stepped back, his expression guarded.

'I must go. I told my mother I wouldn't be long—she'll have a meal ready…' Her voice was rapid, rather breathless. 'Don't worry about the cottage after all—I'll probably be looking at lots of properties before I make a decision.'

He nodded quickly. 'I think that's very wise. It would be wrong to jump into anything without sounding out the market.'

As Sean drove her back Emma reflected wryly that the last thing she should be thinking of was moving next door to Sean Casey. Hadn't she made up her mind that she disliked the man since the first moment she'd met him that morning? Did she really want to be his neighbour? Admittedly, he was drop-dead gorgeous but she was learning rather quickly that she could stray into dangerous emotional territory when she was too close to him—and she had learned from experience that romance and she didn't mix. She flicked a glance at his profile—his expression was remote, unfathomable, so perhaps he was having second thoughts about her living near him too!

Sean dropped her off at her house, refusing an offer to come in.

'See you at work tomorrow,' he said. 'I hope you'll have recovered from all the excitement by then!'

He drove away, flicking an eye in the rear-view mirror, seeing Emma's slender figure silhouetted against the doorway, and smacked the steering-wheel hard with his hand. What the hell had come over him a few minutes ago in the cottage? Why had he kissed her and, even worse, mentioned the cottage near him was for sale? He didn't want any colleagues living next door to him—he wanted space in his off-duty time. He'd grown to treasure his solitude, living anonymously next to people he didn't know, who asked no questions. Of course, he reflected, that had been before he'd met Emma Fulford—was it only nine hours ago? Now his impulsive behaviour might have ruined his precious solitude—and all because, he thought angrily, he had allowed himself to be swept away by a pair of amber eyes, the colour of light sherry!

Since the moment they'd met that morning, Emma had not been far from his thoughts. She had taken him unawares and had pulled him into the real world of sex and the powerful feelings of attraction he could not indulge in now. At the moment there were other things in his life that demanded his attention.

He crashed the gears in annoyance as he turned the car into his little drive. He should have kept his mouth shut—the last person in the world he wanted to get involved with was Emma Fulford. It had been a shock when he had discovered that they were going to be working together, and a double irony that of all people he should be featured with her in the local paper. He needed to keep her at a distance, professionally and socially.

CHAPTER THREE

SUDDENLY all was chaos in Casualty. As so often happened, there had been a quiet period before the storm, and at half past ten the department had been empty. Some of the staff were taking the opportunity to have a coffee, or an illegal cigarette behind the bins outside. Staff Nurse Bill Taylor was checking the drugs cupboard and Sister Tania Cornish was showing a junior nurse how to give intramuscular injections.

Emma watched Sean sitting in the corner of the staff-room, reading a medical paper on diabetes management. It had been several days since the waterskiing accident and Sean had not mentioned it since—she got the impression that he was avoiding her as much as she was trying to steer clear of him. And nothing could suit her more, she thought defiantly.

Perhaps she had imagined the charged atmosphere between them that afternoon in Sean's cottage—after all, he had just brushed her cheek with his lips in acknowledgement of her part in the rescue of the water-skier. It probably meant nothing to him. She shivered in fresh remembrance of the enormous physical attraction she'd felt for Sean, every nerve ending responding to his closeness—and how dangerous was that? To begin with, wasn't he just the type of man she disliked, with his touch of arrogance when displeased? But even more to the point, she had barely got over the terrible mistake she'd made over a man in the past. No one was perfect, but surely experience had taught her that if a man had a flaw—forget him!

Then the phones started clamouring, ambulances arrived in force and suddenly there were twelve people with different diagnoses and treatments. Scaffolding had fallen down in a main shopping area of Carrfield and there were several injured pedestrians and two people working on the building had serious injuries. This was typical of the casualty department—impossible to predict what might happen. And when all hell let loose after a period of inactivity, one had to force oneself into top gear and get the adrenalin pumping.

'Emma, can you go into the small theatre and help Sean? A patient there has multiple injuries,' said Connie, her voice brusque with the tension of organising staff to deal with the victims.

It was ironic, thought Emma as she dodged trolleys and oxygen cylinders being wheeled to various cubicles, that she should have to work so closely with Sean when each of them were doing their best to avoid the other!

Sean looked up as she came in. He was listening through his stethoscope to the chest of an inert figure, ominously quiet on the bed in front of him. Tania was setting up a drip and attaching the patient to various monitors.

'We need bloods for cross-matching.' Sean's voice was brisk and authoritative. 'This young woman's got multiple fractures and a piece of steel from the scaffolding's pierced her arm. She's going to need surgery, possible skin graft.'

'Another shopper caught in the scaffold collapse? Poor thing…'

'She was actually one of the scaffolders—her helmet saved her from further damage.'

Emma looked down at the victim's face—she was in her twenties, the pallor of her skin chalky white above the sheet she was lying on. With a frisson of horror Emma realised that the steel was still in the woman's arm, sticking out of the limb obscenely like a revolting growth.

She took a deep breath. 'I'll take these bloods and make sure Theatre's ready. Is the surgeon on standby?'

Sean nodded. 'Paul Blakeney's on his way down with the anaesthetist. From the difficulty I've had getting an airway in, I think her larynx is swollen—she's probably had a blow to the neck.'

'At least she's out of it at the moment,' murmured Tania. 'Poor woman's in a mess.'

'What are her obs, Sister?'

'BP 80 over 50, dropping, pulse thready...'

'BP may go up with the drip—can you increase that slightly, please?'

The girl stirred slightly and groaned, her voice muffled through the oxygen mask.

'Emma, can you give her 2.5 milligrams of diamorphine—she seems to be coming round a bit. Hopefully she'll be in surgery soon, so I don't want to give her too much.'

Sean turned as a man came through the door. 'Ah, Paul, glad to see you. This young lady's very battered—X-rays show hairline fracture of the femur and a fractured fibula. And on top of that, this piece of metal stuck in her arm.'

The surgeon looked closely at the X-ray hooked over the viewing screen and gave a low whistle. 'We're going to need John Burton, I think. She needs more than one person working on her at once. We must get that metal out of her arm—probably a lot of nerve damage there. Get her down to Theatre a.s.a.p. What are her obs?' he asked.

'She's reasonably stable,' said Tania, who had been monitoring the blood pressure and blood oxygen levels. 'Her BP's gone up slightly…85 over 60. Pulse is stronger.'

'OK, then—let's go!'

The patient was taken out of the small theatre to the big operating theatre. Sean pulled off his rubber gloves and flung them into a waste bin, then stretched his long back stiffly.

'That was pretty nasty—she won't be going up scaffolding for a while.' He grimaced, rubbing the small of his back. 'I could do with a coffee—any chance?'

Connie put her head round the door. 'Not yet, I'm afraid. We've got a little girl here with a nasty bump on her head—she's just been brought out from under the scaffolding. We don't know her name—her mother may be among the injured.'

A small figure on the trolley was wheeled in, and Emma caught her breath. The child was no more than five years old with a mass of blonde curls, now matted with blood, her eyes closed and her face pallid. An ugly purple bruise showed swollen and grotesque on her forehead and two plump little arms were flung out on either side of her. A swell of sympathy for the tiny vulnerable figure on the large trolley seemed to fill the room and the staff clustered round her almost protectively. Tania immediately put in an intravenous line and hooked her up to a monitor.

Sean pursed his lips as he looked at the blow to her head. 'I think we're going to need a CAT scan—she may have a fractured skull. How are her reactions, Emma?'

Emma pulled up the little girl's eyelid to expose the pupil and shone her penlight into them. 'Pupils are reacting,' she said. Then she ran a pencil under the child's small foot and it curled immediately. 'Plantar reaction OK.' She bent down and stroked the pale little face. 'Is your head sore, lovey?'

The eyelids fluttered open for a second, and the child's lip quivered. 'Mummy…where's Mummy?'

'At least she heard you,' Sean murmured, meeting Emma's eyes in mutual compassion. He held the child's little hand in his, his voice very gentle. 'Don't worry, sweetheart—your mummy's not far away. We just want to make your poorly head better. Can you tell me your name?'

The child looked at him in a bewildered way, but as he stroked her hand she seemed to relax slightly. She focussed on him for a minute, then she seemed to gather courage and in a small cracked voice whispered, 'Bethany.'

'Thank you, Bethany. You are being a brave little girl.'

Emma watched Sean's hands stroking the child's face, his concentration completely given over to his small patient. She was learning quite a lot of things about this man, she reflected, and one of them was his ability to deal with children.

Bethany clutched his hand, and looked round at the alien faces around her. Her voice wobbled piteously. 'Want to go home…don't like it here.'

'Soon, Bethany, my love, when you're feeling better,' soothed Sean.

Emma said quietly, 'Should we sedate her? She's not going to like the scan much, is she?'

'Ring George Bowers in Paediatrics—he needs to come and look at Bethany. I feel a little out of my depth with little ones—feel I'm treading on eggshells where their treatment's concerned.'

Connie slipped into the room and came over to look at the child. 'Poor little mite,' she said. 'How's she doing?'

'It's possible she may have a skull fracture,' replied Sean, 'but she's stable and her reactions are OK.'

Connie drew Sean and Emma away from the bed. Her face looked tired, the strain of the last hour showing. 'I'm afraid to say one of the victims has just died on us—multiple internal injuries. We did our best. The thing is, we think it could be this little one's grandmother—probably the person she was with in the shopping centre.'

They looked in horror at Connie. 'Was the mother there as well?' asked Emma falteringly.

'We don't think so—everyone's accounted for, and most of them are minor injuries, friends out together for the morning. We think Bethany's gran was alone with her.'

'Can we contact the mother?' Sean's voice was terse.

'The police are on it now. The grandmother is a Mrs Tyson, which we got from the pension book in her handbag. She also had a photo of Bethany and a young woman—we think she's the mum, she's very like Bethany. The young woman won't know of the grandmother's death yet.'

'My God,' muttered Emma. 'I know it goes with the job, but I hate this part of it...'

Sean nodded grimly. 'Not good, is it, having to break horrible news?'

There was a cough from the doorway and the receptionist's anxious face peered round.

'Dr Casey, the mother of the little girl is here—she's very distressed. She'd gone to meet her mother at the shopping centre when she came across the accident.'

Her words were interrupted by a high keening sound and running footsteps in the corridor. 'My baby...my baby, where is she? Let me see her, for God's sake!'

'Sounds like the mother now,' muttered Sean. 'I think I'd better see what's happening and try and calm her down before she sees Bethany. Keep that drip going.'

He strode out of the room with Katie, and Emma and Tania talked soothingly to the little patient, trying to keep the child from getting too upset. Bethany gave a huge sob occasionally, her lower lip trembling, and she clutched Tania's hand.

'At least she doesn't seem drowsy,' murmured Emma. She went to a cupboard and brought out a rather battered-looking rag doll. 'Look, darling,' she said, holding the doll in front of Bethany. 'The dolly's called Jemima and she's got a bad head like you—I'm going to put a big plaster on it so that she'll get better.'

Bethany's sobs subsided, her attention held as she watched Emma bandage the doll. By the time the mother was brought in by Sean, her little daughter looked quite calm and was clutching the doll possessively.

'This is Tracy, Bethany's mother.' said Sean. 'I've

told her that the paediatrician will be coming to see Bethany and we're going to check that there's no skull fracture or other damage with a CAT scan.'

Tracy looked round anxiously, her bewildered and shocked expression typical of those suddenly confronted with places and emotions totally alien to them. She was having to adjust very quickly to a nightmare situation.

Sean held her arm comfortingly and led her over to the bed where the small figure of her daughter lay. Tears streamed down the young mother's face.

'Bethany... Oh, my poor little baby...' She bent down and kissed the child's cheek, barely controlling her sobs and clutching Bethany's hand wordlessly. Her daughter's face also crumpled, seeing her mother's distress, and Emma squeezed Tracy's shoulder, trying to prevent the hysteria she felt could overcome the mother.

'Try not to cry for Bethany's sake,' she urged gently. 'We need to keep cheerful for her.'

Tracy nodded and, making a tremendous effort, subdued her sobs and smiled in a watery way at Bethany. 'You're Mummy's brave little angel, aren't you?' she whispered. 'You'll soon be better.'

Sean was talking in a quiet voice to George Bowers, the paediatrician, who had just arrived, giving him the details they knew so far of Bethany's condition, explaining the circumstances. George was a big bluff, teddy bear of a man, with twinkling eyes and an ill-fitting suit, and not at all intimidating.

'Will Bethany be all right?' Tracy whispered.

'We haven't done the scan yet of her skull,' he said cautiously, 'but, given that she seems alert, I hope we'll have her back home very soon. But I want to keep her under observation for at least forty-eight hours. We'll take her up to the children's ward now and if you would come with us, I'm sure someone will find you a nice hot cup of tea!'

Tracy looked sadly at Tania and Emma. 'It's my fault, you know. If I hadn't been going for an interview for a job, her gran wouldn't have had to take Bethany to the shops. I didn't need to go for a job—I could have managed on Social Security. If I had been looking after her, none of this would have happened.'

Emma took both her hands. 'It isn't your fault at all, Tracy—you must never think that. Now, you go to the ward and walk beside Bethany—she can take the little doll with her. Would you like that, sweetheart?'

Bethany nodded and clutched the doll closely to her as she was wheeled away.

'I take it Tracy hasn't been told yet of her mother's death?' said Tania as she folded a clean sheet over the bed ready for the next patient.

'I believe Connie told her,' replied Sean. 'She's got a lot to cope with.'

He began to write up Bethany's notes, and Emma helped Tania push the equipment out of the way. After the drama of the last half-hour it was blessedly peaceful.

A few minutes later there was a bang as the swing doors were pushed roughly open and a harsh voice shouted, 'Where the hell's my daughter? What's that little bitch being doing to her?'

They all wheeled round in amazement. A thick-set young man with tattooed arms and pierced brows, nose and lip stood in the doorway, looking belligerently at them.

'Excuse me? Did you want something?' Sean's voice was cold. 'If you're not a patient, you shouldn't be in this area.'

'Too right I want something. My kid's in here somewhere and I need to see her.'

Sean moved over to the man, towering over him intimidatingly. 'And what's your daughter's name?'

'Bethany. I was in the pub opposite when the scaffolding collapsed—I saw the whole thing happen. Bethany was hurt just because her stupid mother couldn't look after her properly. Where is she? I know she was in here before.'

Sean put his hand up as if to interrupt the flow of words. 'And you're name is...?'

'Brett Turner.' He thrust his chin towards Sean with a sneer. 'Just because I don't see Bethany's mother doesn't mean I can't see my own kid. I could have looked after her better than that old grandmother.'

Sean folded his arms and looked down at the man stonily, and Emma was suddenly rather glad that he had as tough an aggressive streak in him as Brett Turner.

'No one could have predicted that the scaffolding would fall. Bethany's grandmother was killed because of a terrible accident, but hopefully Bethany is going to be all right.'

For a second Brett looked taken aback, then he psyched himself up again, squaring his shoulders, and said sullenly, 'I didn't know Tracy's mum had bought it. Anyway they'll get compensation—someone's to blame. Nobody's going to get away with that. Now, where's my kid? It's my right to see her.'

Sean turned to Tania and said in a low voice, 'Sister Cornish, perhaps you'd like to go and discuss the matter with Bethany's mother? We need to know the situation here.'

'What's there to discuss?' asked the man, pushing his head forward aggressively.

'I'm thinking of your little girl,' replied Sean smoothly. 'She must be kept very quiet. She doesn't need parents quarrelling over who was to blame...your, er, wife is understandably distraught over her little girl and the death of her mother. She needs a lot of support at the moment.'

Emma stepped forward. 'I'm sure you'll be able to see Bethany soon—she's probably having a scan at the moment anyway. If you go and wait in the reception area we'll try and find out what's happening.'

The man scowled, but he followed Emma out of the room. 'I'm not being fobbed off,' he growled. 'I want to see Bethany—and pronto!'

'We'll do our best,' said Emma coolly, doing her best to keep a professional detachment in her voice when she really longed to say something extremely rude to him. 'Wait here and you'll be told of Bethany's progress as soon as we can.'

'There'd better be some info pretty soon, or I'll be onto the authorities—I have my rights as a parent too!'

Later that morning Emma went to the staffroom—it had been a tough few hours with medical emergencies as diverse as a child with a small bead stuck in his ear to an old lady who'd been mugged. Tania and Sean were both pouring themselves large mugs of coffee, and Emma collapsed into a chair with a groan.

'Wow,' she sighed. 'Why the hell do we do this job?'

Sean grinned. 'For love of humanity, of course…and the thanks we get from a grateful public. Talking of which, how did you get on with Bethany's charming father?'

'He gave me a lecture on parental rights, got a bit angry when he was told he'd have to wait some time. What on earth made Tracy go for a guy like him?'

Tania shrugged. 'One of the eternal mysteries of life. Ah, well, I must go and sort out Zak—that porter seems to disappear more than he's here. I think he's got a glamorous girlfriend on the surgical ward. By the way, talking of glamour…' She rummaged in her handbag for a second and looked up at Sean and Emma with a mischievous smile. 'How's this for a star shot?'

She pulled a newspaper out of her bag and held it up to them. Emma found herself looking at a full-page spread of a photo of her and Sean on the beach after the waterskiing accident.

'Behold!' Tania said gleefully. 'Front-page news on the *Carrfield Argos*—the heroes of the hour. I think it should be on the noticeboard!'

'Oh, heavens,' squeaked Emma. 'That towel barely covers me!'

'Don't you make a lovely couple?' remarked Tania impishly as she swept out.

Sean and Emma looked at each other with wry smiles. 'I suppose that we'll be the talk of the hospital soon,' remarked Sean drily. He picked up the paper, which Tania had thrown on the chair, and studied the photo closely. 'However,' he added, looking at her with a grin, 'you at least are very photogenic!'

Emma scowled crossly. 'I didn't realise that the thing would be printed on the first page—nor did I realise that I'd look semi-naked!'

Sean threw back his head and laughed. 'As the young journalist said, the circulation's probably gone up tremendously.' He looked at her more seriously. 'It could have ended in tragedy if you hadn't been there, you know.'

'Good job you were there too. I wonder how the young man is? I meant to check but life's been a bit hectic.'

Sean nodded. 'I did actually go and see him—he's on Surgical and had to have a splenectomy. He's doing all right.' He looked at her pale face and smiled kindly at her as if aware that the morning had taken its toll. 'Look, how about some coffee? I guess you could do with something after this morning's dramas.'

The atmosphere between them seemed to have lightened, as if their mutual amused embarrassment at the publishing of the photo had relaxed them, and Emma sipped the hot coffee gratefully. The stand-off both of them had been maintaining seemed to have disappeared. Working closely with someone and keeping a distance had been awkward and difficult—perhaps now they could act normally with each other. She looked at Sean's athletic frame draped over one of the sagging armchairs. She'd have to remember to regard him as purely a colleague and not as a drop-dead gorgeous male who set warning bells jangling inside her every time he came close!

He was looking at her quizzically. 'Any luck yet on the property front?'

'No, I've been to every local agent and there's nothing of the size or in the price range I want,' Emma sighed. 'What's worse, my brother and his child are moving in with my mother next week—he's divorced and is going to help my mother with her B and B plans. I can't say that he and I get on very well when we're under the same roof, and I need my own place urgently.'

Sean pulled a piece of paper out of his jacket pocket. 'I was given this last night by the young man who is selling the cottage I mentioned to you—it's the particulars of the property, and the sale price seems reasonable.'

'I didn't see it in any of the agents I went to,' said Emma.

'He wants a private sale—doesn't want to pay agents' fees—but he gave me a key to keep an eye on the place. If you're still interested, I could take you round some time.'

'You might not like a colleague living so near to you.'

He gave a sudden chuckle. 'Perhaps I feel that it's better the devil I know!'

She smiled. 'Well, then, yes, I would love to see it—when you've time to show me, of course.'

'Fine,' said Sean standing up and putting his mug on the side. 'No time like the present. What about tomorrow evening on your way home from work? I'll meet you at my place and take you there.'

Emma left the room and Sean picked up the newspaper and looked at the photograph again. His lips curved into a faint smile—it was idiotic, completely mad, but after only a few days of knowing Emma he wasn't able to stop thinking about her. All his instincts had told him she hadn't liked him at all when they'd met, but he could not help himself. She was so darned beautiful, glossy auburn hair that curled into soft tendrils round face, large tawny eyes and, as was only too evident from the photograph, a curvaceous sexy figure.

It was true that he liked his own anonymous living space but, dammit, he realised that he wanted her to live near him, to get to know her better, and if that meant his privacy was invaded, he'd welcome it!

The past few years had been tough, but surely he deserved to live a little now, Sean told himself bitterly. The last person he would have wished to have fallen for was Professor Fulford's daughter—but it had happened. And after all, it wasn't her fault that her father had ruined his parents' lives and consequently affected Sean's so cruelly.

CHAPTER FOUR

EMMA was much later getting to Sean's than she'd intended. The admission of a woman with an ectopic pregnancy and the arrangements that had needed to be put in place for her surgery had gone way over Emma's shift time—she felt hot, dishevelled and emotionally drained. As she waited for Sean to answer the door she could see her reflection in the window and pulled a face at her frazzled image. The hair she'd pulled back neatly from her face with two clips into a chignon that morning was rapidly escaping from its moorings, and the light make-up she'd applied was now a thing of the past.

The door opened and Sean stood there dressed in jeans and a blue open-necked shirt. Emma's heart thumped. Out of the formality of his work clothes he looked so much younger, more approachable—and incredibly attractive! Living by the sea had given him a light tan and it made his eyes seem startlingly blue, his smile whiter. She took a deep breath—she must forget about his good looks and the tingling feeling she experienced when she was near him. Last time she'd been at this cottage she'd been set alight by his brief kiss: it had awakened feelings she thought she'd never experience again. And she wasn't going to allow them to resurface!

'Sorry I'm late,' she said lightly.

'I was beginning to think you'd changed your mind,' he remarked. 'Trouble at work?'

'A bit chaotic—an ectopic pregnancy brought in just as everyone was changing shifts, and it took ages to find her a bed.'

Sean's glance took in Emma's pale face, the circles under her eyes. 'What you need,' he said firmly, 'is a pick-me-up—how about my own concoction of elder-flower and apple juice with a splash of something else? Not too alcoholic, but quite refreshing—we don't want you making rash decisions about this cottage!'

Emma relaxed slightly and smiled. 'Sounds good to me.'

Sean's ecstatic Labrador welcomed her by doing several laps of the little garden and then, at Sean's stern command, lying down whining with pleasure.

'Calm down, Rocket,' said Sean, rubbing the dog's ears. 'You'll give Emma the impression that you haven't seen anyone all day.' He looked up at Emma. 'Actually, he has two walks a day from an elderly patient of mine who adores him so he gets more exercise than I do!'

The dog lay down beside Emma and looked up at her with liquid brown eyes, wagging his tail—the mention of a walk obviously gave him the idea that that was what Emma was there for!

Emma stroked him. 'He's a lovely animal. Perhaps if I buy this cottage I could get a dog. I've always longed to have one, but have never lived in a suitable place since I left home.'

'Talking of the cottage, I've got the keys and all the information about it here,' Sean said, taking an envelope out of a small desk. 'The man who's selling it is called Arthur Lucas, the son of the old man who lived here. You read it while I get that drink I promised you.'

When he went out Emma looked with interest at the personal items around the room that reflected something of Sean's private life…a cricket ball and bat in a corner, a bookcase filled with a medley of sporting books, some travel books and the odd medical tome. On a small table by the window were a few photographs. One was of a man with dark hair and striking features—probably Sean's father, he was so like him. There was another of a slim, pretty woman who was possibly Sean's mother, holding a little boy by the hand and smiling happily into the camera.

When Sean returned with the drinks, she gestured towards the photographs.

'I'm sure those photos must be of your parents. You are very like your father, and I take it the little boy in the photo with the young woman is you and your mother—she's very beautiful.'

He handed her the drink, and nodded. 'Yes, they are my parents—the photos were taken a long time ago, of course.'

'And do they live near here?' asked Emma politely, sipping her drink. It tasted very refreshing—and the splash of something else Sean had mentioned went straight to Emma's empty stomach rather pleasantly!

There was a second when Emma caught a fleeting stricken look on his face, then he'd composed himself, his expression calm and under control. 'My mother died some time ago—and, no, my father doesn't live near here at the moment.'

'I'm sorry about your mother—it's awful to lose a parent,' she said quietly. 'Although my father and I didn't really get on, it was horrible when he died—a chapter ending so abruptly.'

Sean nodded. 'These things happen...and, yes, I've taken some time to get over it.'

There was something about his voice that discouraged further discussion and Emma tried to turn the conversation to something more upbeat. 'And is your father a medical man?'

Sean shook his head. 'No,' he said shortly. 'He was an engineer—but he's retired now.' He lifted the jug of his special mix and looked at her enquiringly. 'Another glass before we go?'

Emma shook her head. 'It's delicious, but I have to drive, remember, and make some sensible decisions!'

'Then let's go and see what you think of it!'

The cottage was like a doll's house, thought Emma, looking in delight at its grey shingled roof and pink-washed walls. It was rather like a house a child might have drawn—a door in the middle and bay windows on either side.

Sean unlocked the door and they went in, stepping immediately into the living room. It smelt musty, slightly damp, and peeling wallpaper hung from the walls. A couple of old prints hung at crazy angles over the fireplace—nothing had been done to it for a long time, and yet there was a comfortable and cosy air about it.

'Needs a bit of work,' remarked Sean, gazing round. He went up to the window and parted the ragged curtains drawn across the window. 'A graveyard for dead flies here—I don't think the old fellow had bothered much about the house for some time, and I suspect the guttering and windows need renewing.'

'I don't care,' said Emma. 'It's basically a lovely room. Look at those bay windows—I could sit there and feel I was almost on the shore! A lick of paint could make all the difference!'

'You're an optimist,' observed Sean drily. 'There's probably quite a few problems—I wonder what the damp course is like?'

Emma made a face. 'Don't be such a Jonah.' She looked out at the sea—the wind had got up and today it was fairly rough, the breakers crashing onto the shore in a cloud of creamy foam about two hundred yards away. 'Look at that marvellous view—who could ever tire of that?' she exclaimed.

Sean pursed his lips. 'So what happens when there's a storm? You could find you were flooded rather quickly—you need very good advice on that, you know!'

'Well, the place still seems to be standing after over a century,' Emma said lightly, 'so it can't happen often.' She looked at him pertly, lifting her chin and folding her arms challengingly. 'I don't think you really want me to come here at all, do you? That's why you're raising all these objections! You've had second thoughts about me moving in. Well, I like my own space as well, so I assure you I'll keep my distance.'

The low evening sun streamed through the windows and caught Emma's hair in a golden light, the escaping tendrils like a halo round her head, the chignon emphasising her high cheekbones and wide tawny eyes. Her stance was provocative—not deliberately so, Sean thought, but he caught his breath momentarily as he gazed at her. Had she any idea just how desirable she looked?

'Don't be ridiculous,' he said huskily. 'I told you before—I've thought it over, and I don't mind at all. I don't want you to keep your distance. I hope we can become…friendly neighbours.'

There was something in the way his eyes looked at her that made Emma's stomach feel as if a flight of butterflies had started to flutter inside her stomach. The room seemed to close in on them slightly, and she was suddenly very aware that there were just the two of them alone again together. Too reminiscent of the other day in his cottage, she thought in sudden panic.

'Shall we look round the rest of the place?' she said quickly. 'There's a little outhouse apparently that could be used to extend the kitchen, and I ought to see the upstairs.'

Eventually they went up the narrow little stairs that led directly off the kitchen. There was one quite large bedroom, one tiny room and a bathroom. Emma peered round the bathroom door and started to laugh.

'I think the bath's big enough at any rate!' she said. 'I don't know how they got it in here!'

She pointed to the huge Victorian bath that stood on curved legs with enormous taps and a telephone-like shower at one end.

Sean grinned. 'We could both fit into that bath quite easily—and use up about five tankfuls of hot water.'

Emma suddenly had a quick and vivid vision of Sean and herself naked in the bath together, both of them covered in soap, lying against each other—and a shiver of excitement and alarm crackled through her. She closed her eyes for a second, almost feeling his slippery skin against hers, his hands wandering sensually over her… She drew in a deep breath. What was the matter with her? She seemed to be consumed by erotic thoughts of herself and Sean, nervous when he came too near, thinking of him when he wasn't there. She flicked a guilty look at him. Could he tell how out of control her imagination was, and just what she was picturing?

He was studying her expression gravely. 'Penny for them? You seem deep in thought.'

'I…I was just imagining what I could do with this bathroom….'

That was so close to the truth that she almost started to giggle. She turned it into a sharp cough.

'You OK? You look a little flushed. It is a bit stuffy up here—perhaps you need some fresh air?'

'Yes—it is getting a little warm, and I think I've seen everything I need to. Shall we go?'

There was a sudden gust of wind at the windows which rattled alarmingly, and then the sound of crashing masonry outside.

'What on earth was that?'

Sean pulled back the torn blind over the window and they peered outside. A large section of guttering lay forlornly in the small garden and a few tiles were scattered around.

'What did I tell you?' remarked Sean. 'The place needs a bit doing to it!'

Emma looked up at him, frowning. 'Perhaps you're right—I am being too optimistic, and it's too far gone to do much with, but I do love the place.'

'The price seems reasonable. You could probably

afford to do quite a bit to it. The thing is, can you picture yourself at home here?'

'Definitely! I have fallen in love with it. Would you think I was mad if I made an offer subject to the surveyor's report?'

Sean patted his trouser pocket. 'You can ring Arthur Lucas now if you like—I've got my mobile here. His number's on the information pack I gave you. Go downstairs and make the call. Offer him less than the asking price—after all, there is a lot of work to be done on the place. I'll go outside for a minute and see where that guttering's fallen down from.'

A few minutes later Sean came in from his inspection. Emma had just finished her phone call, and she turned to him with shining eyes and almost danced towards him, clapping her hands.

'You'll never guess, Sean, he's accepted my offer—seemed relieved to get rid of the cottage. Isn't that exciting? So, subject to contract, I can't wait to move in! I can't believe it's been so easy!'

Sean laughed, catching her dancing figure in his arms and twirling her round. He was caught up in her euphoria, and she revelled in sharing that excitement with him, hugging him close to her.

He put her down gently, still holding her so close to him that they were standing hip to hip, her soft breasts against his body, and his face a hair's breadth away from hers. They smiled at each other for a second, then quite abruptly Sean put his hands on either side of her face and kissed her fully on her mouth. Fuelled by her elation over the cottage, all sensible feelings of restraint seemed to fly out of Emma's head. She wound her arms round his neck and arched her back in instant response, pressing against him, allowing him to tease open her lips, then shivering as he moved his mouth down to the delicious little hollow in her neck with tantalising butterfly kisses.

'I didn't know what I was letting myself in for when I got into that taxi!' he whispered.

She twisted round in his arms and looked at him, startled and brought back to reality by the intensity of his voice. This was getting dangerous—he was assuming too much and she was giving him all the wrong messages.

'We mustn't let this get too far, Sean. We've only known each other a few days, and I'm not ready to...' Her voice trailed off helplessly, trying to find suitable words.

'What aren't you ready to do?' asked Sean, his voice muffled as he kissed the nape of her neck.

'Get involved. Not yet... If I'm to live so close to you, it could lead to all kinds of complications if we...well, become too...'

'Entangled?' he said teasingly. 'Don't be such a worrier, Emma—things will work out.'

She tried to pull away from him. 'No, no, I can't—I'm not ready to get involved.' She gave a wry smile. 'Anyway, you aren't the type of man I go for at all...'

He raised his brows, his eyes amused but questioning. 'And what kind of man is that?'

She was silent, wrestling with her emotions, trying to still the voice in her head that told her that he was *just* the kind of man she wanted. Her initial reactions to Sean Casey had done a complete about-turn!

'To be honest, I don't think I can commit to any man now...please, understand.'

He frowned. 'For goodness' sake—why not?' He drew her gently to him again, one hand stroking the soft curves of her body. 'I've never heard such nonsense,' he murmured. He looked down at her, his eyes sweeping over her upturned face. 'You know, Emma, you don't realise it, but you are unbelievably beautiful.'

She pulled away from him and moved towards the window, her voice surprisingly sharp. 'Please, don't say that sort of thing, Sean. I don't want to hear it.'

He looked at her, startled, slightly shocked by the tone of her voice. 'Why not? It's true.'

She bit her lip, then said slowly, 'They're only words, words I've heard before. So easy to say—half the time they aren't meant!'

'You've been hurt, Emma. From what you say, this old boyfriend sounds an insincere rat. We're not all like that, you know!'

'You don't know anything about my past life, Sean. I've been a fool and it's taught me not to believe everything one hears. Believe me…' Emma's tone hardened. 'I'm not sure that I need anyone now, and I don't think I have the capacity to make anyone happy.'

'That's nonsense,' said Sean roughly. 'Everyone has to get over things, put prejudices behind them. If they don't, they might never find happiness.'

Emma looked at him wryly. 'So you speak from experience, do you?'

He bunched his fists tightly in his pockets. 'Oh, yes, I speak from experience, but gradually I'm coming to terms with what happened to me and my family—and I'm damn well not letting it ruin my life now.' He moved nearer and said gently, 'I don't want to trap you into anything you don't want, Emma, but don't tell me you didn't enjoy what we've just been doing, because I won't believe you!'

And how embarrassing this was, thought Emma, feeling her face redden. Of course she'd responded to his kisses, she wasn't made of steel. She'd enjoyed every damned crazy second of it! Even thinking about his lips trailing fire down her neck made the butterflies in her stomach start their mad fluttering again.

'I'm sorry—I didn't mean to lead you on. I was just so ecstatic about the cottage and everything I got carried away.' She looked at him almost pleadingly. 'Coming back to Carrfield, I feel much happier than I have for a long time—but I need my space, time to adjust. Can you understand?'

He looked at her for a long silent minute, then shrugged. 'If that's what you want. But I don't believe it for a second.' He bent his head towards her and kissed her gently on her mouth again. 'At least let's be good friends!'

Dammit, thought Emma as she drove home, her lips tingling from his touch, that's just what I do want him to do—and much, much more! A shiver of fear ran through her. Would it all end in a broken heart again?

Sean poured himself a large whisky and sat in the window of his living room, looking out at the dramatic sea, huge breakers now crashing on the shore, the spray as it hit the rocks spectacular as the evening sun reached the horizon. He stroked Rocket gently as the dog sat by him attentively, hoping against hope he'd get another walk.

'You know, old boy,' Sean murmured, 'if anyone

had told me I'd have anything to do with anyone connected to Robert Fulford a few weeks ago, I'd have said they were barmy!' He took a deep sip of whisky and leaned back reflectively in his chair. 'Am I mad to think Emma and I are meant for each other? I tell you something, Rocket, I'm not going to let her go easily!'

The dog panted and looked at him with adoring eyes, as if to say anything Sean said was fine with him.

Sean stood up and stretched. 'You agree with me, Rocket? Well, all I've got to do is convince her of that!' He opened the door that led out of the sitting room and gave a low whistle. 'Come on, then, boy, let's have that walk while I think out my strategy!'

Emma rubbed her aching back—she'd been bending over a patient for ten minutes, trying to remove slivers of glass from the cut on his arm where a shattered beer glass had made contact in a pub fight.

'There you are, Wayne,' she said. 'I've done my best with those stitches—should be a nice straight scar! Try and keep out of the way of flying glasses in future!'

The young man scowled. 'I'm going to hit him where it hurts next time I see him. He'll be begging for mercy by the time I've finished.' He peered anxiously down at his arm now covered with a dressing. 'What about the tattoo—has it ruined it?'

'No, you're all right,' said Emma gravely. 'I managed to put the stitches along the dragon's spiked neck—I don't think you'll notice at all after a few months!'

Wayne grunted and ambled out, and Tania, checking the instrument tray, gave a smothered gurgle of laughter. 'Good job it wasn't his back.' She grinned. 'He had a large tattoo of a rather big lady right across his shoulder blades and down to his you-know-where—I don't know where you'd have disguised the scar there!'

Connie put her head round the door. 'What are you two giggling about?' she asked.

'Just a moment of light relief, Dr Gorton,' said Tania. 'Emma's been refining her artistic skills on a young man's tattoo!'

'We all need light relief,' said Connie gloomily. 'I'm afraid I'll have to bring you down to earth, Emma—a young woman in the small theatre. Sean's already there, assessing her. Her partner's beaten her up and her face is a terrible mess—can you assist? Tania, you're needed in number six—a little boy with a broken arm needs plastering.'

It was the first time Emma had worked closely with Sean for a few days—in fact, since the night she'd looked round Pebble Cottage with him. As she walked briskly to the small theatre she couldn't help the thud her heart gave as the familiar sensation of unknown excitement associated with Sean fluttered in her stomach. Sternly she told herself to concentrate on the matter in hand. Sean was a professional colleague—she'd got to put out of her mind the vivid picture she had in her mind of them kissing passionately in Pebble Cottage!

Sean was gowned and had his mask on and was sitting on a chair opposite the patient, peering closely at her face, inspecting her injuries through a large magnifying glass.

'That you, Dr Fulford?' he said, without turning round. 'This is Doreen Cullen, brought in with facial injuries. Could you have a look and tell me what you think about this cheek wound?'

Doreen was a small woman with big scared eyes that watched Emma warily. She lay on the operating table with the head end raised to lessen tension on her facial tissues. Her face was swollen and blotched, one eye was virtually closed and there was a curious serrated gash on her cheek.

Through puffy bruised lips she whispered defensively, 'Len didn't mean to do it—it was the drink that got to him. I did something to annoy him, see?'

Emma let out a deep breath—it wasn't her job to be judgmental, but she felt a wave of anger at Doreen's passive acceptance of her boyfriend's brutality and that somehow she was to blame for what he'd done to her.

'It's not your fault he's used you as a punchbag,' she murmured as she used a torch and the magnifying glass to see how deep the wound was. 'Does he do this to you often?'

'Only sometimes when he's had the odd drink...'

Emma's eyes met Sean's, gazing at her sardonically over his mask, and she sighed. No good talking about the culpability of Doreen's boyfriend—from experience she knew that Doreen would probably stick up for him, no matter what. Her job and Sean's was to reassure their patient, try and instill in the frightened woman that she was in safe hands and that she could relax now she was out of danger.

'Do you know how this cut on your cheek was made?' Emma enquired gently.

'A kitchen knife—one for cutting bread.' Two big tears welled up in Doreen's eyes and she gave a choked sob. 'He's not taken a knife to me before....'

'Never mind, love. Dr Casey will soon have you stitched up, and your face will look as good as new eventually. Give it time.' She turned to Sean and murmured, 'It looks pretty deep and ragged.'

'I know,' replied Sean getting up and folding his arms as he gazed down at the young girl's face assessingly. 'Unfortunately, Mr Beavis, the plastic surgeon, has just been involved in a car accident himself, would you believe? But I think we ought to do something about this wound a.s.a.p. before it has a chance to build up infection. Fortunately Doreen was brought in very soon after the assault so the closure should present a good appearance.'

Emma nodded. 'Bacteria can double every six hours in a wound,' she explained to Doreen. 'And the longer it takes to deal with it, the more risk there is of clinical infection, which means the whole thing has to be opened again—and we don't want you left with a jagged scar.'

'Don't worry, Doreen,' said Sean with a grin, looking down at the young woman's apprehensive face. 'I have done this sort of thing before—I did a six-month rotation with Mr Beavis a year ago and he's one of the best teachers there are. I think I've majored in facial knife wounds!' He turned to Emma. 'Better see if there are any other injuries before I start.'

He was right, thought Emma as she palpated the girl's abdomen. In cases of domestic violence there were often body blows that could be overlooked when dealing with the immediate and more apparent facial injury.

'Did he hit your stomach, Doreen? You must have put up a fight.'

'He tried to kick me, but I ran next door...' Doreen's fragile composure cracked and she started to cry properly, putting her hands up to her battered face to try and smother her sobs. 'He said...he said he'd get me next time.'

'Next time?' said Emma.

'He thinks I'm having it off with his friend—but I'm not. He's jealous.'

Again, Sean's eyes met Emma's in cold condemnation of the patient's boyfriend. He patted Doreen's arm comfortingly.

'Don't worry about that now. We're going to start work on this cut so lie back and relax. Dr Fulford, we'll give Doreen some lignocaine to numb her cheek and I shall use an advancement flap to minimise scarring.'

Emma watched Sean start work on the gashed cheek with a degree of admiration. He was painstaking—his concentration absolute as he worked on the wound, careful not to draw the ragged edges too tightly together.

'We've got to adapt this underlying tissue,' he explained in a low voice as he worked, separating the skin from the tissue. 'That will free extra skin to be laid against each side of the wound for closure without tension...don't want to create any sites of infection if we pull the edges inward.'

At last Sean stood up, stretching his back and puffing out his cheeks in relief. 'Whew! What do you think, Dr Fulford?'

'A very neat job, Dr Casey.' Emma smiled down at Doreen. 'In a few months there won't be anything to show—perhaps a very thin line which you can hide with make-up.'

Doreen made an effort at a smile with her swollen lips. 'That's good,' she whispered. 'One of the things Len likes about me is my complexion.'

Sean shook his head in mystification as he pulled off his latex gloves after Doreen had been taken to one of the cubicles. 'It doesn't make sense, does it? She'll probably be back soon with some other adjustments her darling Len has made to her face.' He rubbed his eyes wearily. 'Thank God I've got the weekend off—I'll make good use of it!'

'What will you do?' asked Emma curiously.

'The forecast's good—I think I'll go dolphin-watching in the waters beyond the bay. It's a wonderful sight, seeing them leaping out of the sea. Ever seen them?'

Emma shook her head. 'No. I knew they were in the area, of course.'

'You don't know what you're missing. Why don't you come?' Sean's voice was casual but he looked at her keenly. 'We could take a picnic—perhaps bathe in one of the little coves round the bay afterwards. It's certainly a complete contrast to this place!'

How tempting it was, thought Emma—and how dangerous! Just the two of them in the most intimate of settings, a small boat… How very unwise it would be to go with Sean on such an outing.

'I'd love to,' she said. 'It sounds a marvellous idea!'

'Pick you up at ten o'clock tomorrow, then,' said Sean.

The first part of his strategy seemed to be working, he thought with a smile as he strode down the corridor.

CHAPTER FIVE

THE day was perfect—clear blue sky, the sea as calm as a millpond, the little mini-waves sparkling in the sun and the incredible beauty of the bay with its surrounding hills. Emma scowled at herself in the mirror. Why did it have to be such a gorgeous day—why wasn't it pouring with rain so that the whole thing could be called off?

'You utter fool,' she said sternly to her reflection. 'Agreeing to go with Sean on this "dolphin watch" is just the stupidest thing I could have done. Just the two of us...alone...all day! I must be completely mad!'

Emma sighed as she put the faintest touch of gloss on her lips and pulled her hair back into a ponytail. Too late now to get out of it, but one thing was certain—she was going to sit as far as possible away from Sean in the boat! Hadn't she made it very clear that she didn't want to get involved with anyone? She wasn't going to give him the chance to think she was encouraging any physical contact! She was only going because dolphin-watching sounded so fascinating—they were wonderful creatures and she wanted to find out more about them. And she hoped he understood that.

'You going out, sis?'

Emma jumped and turned round. Charles was standing in the doorway with Ben by his side. He had virtually moved into the house now, and Ben's toys had taken over a large part of the house from the sitting room to the bathroom.

'A colleague is taking me dolphin-watching—I've never done it, and it sounds fun,' she replied. 'Did you want something?'

In her experience, Charles usually wanted some favour.

He said casually, 'I promised I'd take Ben to the little fair at the beach—but I've left my wallet at the old house. You couldn't lend me forty smackers, could you?'

Emma suppressed a sigh and fished out some money, handing it to Charles. He always seemed to have left his wallet somewhere.

He pocketed it, and smiled charmingly. 'Thanks, Emma—you'll get it back very soon, I promise.'

I wonder, thought Emma cynically. She turned to little Ben, a plump and engaging three-year-old.

'Hello, darling,' she said fondly. 'Are you going to go on the swings and roundabouts with Daddy?'

Ben beamed. 'You come too?' he asked hopefully.

'Not today, Ben, but I'll take you with me another time. We'll build sandcastles on the beach.'

'Looks like your date's here,' remarked Charles, peering out of the window. 'Quite a swish car he's got!'

'He's not a date,' said Emma lightly. 'I told you, he's just a colleague.' She bent down and kissed Ben's plump cheek. 'See you later, sweetheart.'

'I don't know if we'll be in luck and see any dolphins,' remarked Sean as he steered the boat slowly along, making as little wake as possible. 'Keep your eyes peeled for any activity.'

Emma sat forward with excited anticipation—it would be wonderful to see the creatures at such close quarters.

'What are the chances?' she said.

'It's pretty hit or miss—sometimes one can see a whole pod or family leaping along and watch them for ages. You can come back half an hour later and they've vanished completely.' He looked at her sternly. 'I hope you've put some high-factor sunscreen on your skin—the sun's really strong out here.'

'Don't worry, I'm plastered in the stuff.' Emma lifted her head back and revelled in the warm salty air on her face, shaking her hair out of its restricting ponytail and allowing the breeze to blow through it. 'This is wonderful. The hospital feels a million miles away.'

Sean laughed, revealing a flash of strong white teeth. 'Well, it's not—there it is, perched high on the cliff. It's really a fantastic building and it has a better view than the Grand Hotel down the road!'

Emma didn't notice the hungry way he was looking at her, taking in the grace of her body as she tilted her face back, her thick auburn hair like a halo round her face. If only she could learn to trust him, not dwell on the man in the past who'd obviously hurt her deeply. Now she looked relaxed and happy—and Sean wanted her to stay that way.

They were heading out to sea beyond the confines of the bay and Sean scanned the area with binoculars.

'Can you see anything?' asked Emma.

'I'm looking for any disturbance in the water—dolphins often travel in a way known as "porpoising"—

that is, swimming through the surface, diving and surging up, sometimes leaping clear of the water. Take the wheel, will you, while I concentrate?'

Emma obediently held the wheel steady. Sean stood up to the side of her—far too close, she thought nervously. He was wearing tattered shorts, and his legs were strong and powerful, like the man himself. She could see the golden hairs on his calves, an old scar across his knee. When he put one hand down to steady himself, she stared down at it—that same hand had made her body tingle with desire just a day or two before, caressing her body with an intimacy that had fired every nerve. Uneasily she shifted in her seat, trying to put some space between herself and the dangerous proximity of Sean's body.

Suddenly he tensed and put one hand up warningly. 'Slow the engine down,' he said. 'Let's just coast along for a while—I think I can see something ahead of us. Can you make out a line of foam about three hundred yards away?'

Emma screwed up her eyes and, yes, she could see the water breaking, and then suddenly a streamlined form leapt out of the water, spinning in the air before it plunged back—then another and another.

She drew in a deep breath of excitement. 'Oh, how fantastic! They're all doing it!'

The spray from their torpedo-like bodies glinted and sparkled as at least twenty dolphins twisted and spun before them. Rainbow-coloured droplets showered around them as several dolphins at a time leapt from the surface of the sea and dived back as cleanly through the water as Olympic divers.

Sean gave a low chuckle. 'They're showing off—

they love to perform when they sense someone's watching them and not threatening them in any way.'

'They seem to be having such fun—look at them splashing with their tails and flippers.' Emma laughed. She breathed a sigh of delight. 'I never thought I'd see anything like this!'

'We've been lucky,' remarked Sean, putting down the binoculars and sitting beside her. 'Just accelerate very gradually.'

He was very close to her, his bare legs brushing against hers, and she felt her heartbeat mimicking the increased speed of the engine revs.

'Won't we frighten them, going faster?' she asked rather breathlessly.

'They sometimes enjoy riding in the waves behind the boat. They get used to the engine noise—look! They're jumping behind us now!'

It was a stunning sight and they watched it in thrilled silence for a quite a while before the dolphins seemed to tire of showing off and gradually stopped surging through the water, disappearing out to sea.

'That was quite wonderful,' Emma breathed.

'Long may it continue,' remarked Sean grimly. 'They're at terrible risk nowadays from oil pollution, sewage and the rubbish people leave on the shore that gets washed out to sea.'

Sean's blue eyes were sombre, and gazing at him Emma suddenly wondered why she had hated him so much when they'd first met. There was so much more to Sean than an arrogant wish to impose his will on others. She was beginning to realise that there was a genuine compassion for others that she hadn't seen at first—all she'd seen on that first day they'd met had been a powerful man who'd seemed to want his own way. She'd had her fill of powerful bullies in the past...but maybe she'd got it wrong with Sean.

He was smiling at her. 'Feeling hungry?' he asked. 'I think we'll make for one of the little coves round the bay before the weather changes. I've got a rather nice white wine that needs to be drunk while it's still cold, and plenty of smoked salmon.'

The inlet he took them to was tiny, with a curving beach of white, almost pink sand. The cliffs rose up high around it, spattered with buttercups and cornflowers, and there was a tangy smell of seaweed in the warm air.

Sean cut the engine and they drifted to shore, then he leapt out and pulled the boat as high as he could, anchoring its rope in the sand. They carried the baskets of food and drink up the shore, and deposited them on a rug under the shelter of a bent tree clinging to the bottom of the cliff.

He turned to her and grinned. 'Swim first—food later!'

Then he pulled off his shorts and shirt, stripping to his bathing trunks and revealing a muscular tanned body. 'Come on,' he urged. 'I'll race you to the sea!'

The bikini Emma was wearing under her cropped trousers was the most modest she could find, but even so she felt a wave of self-consciousness as she stripped down to the bikini and stood by him, extremely aware of just how naked their bodies were—how close they were to each other.

He smiled at her mischievously, his gaze flickering over her in frank admiration. 'You look very fit, Emma.

Is it just an illusion, or are you as athletic as I think you are?'

She flung a towel at him. 'You trying to tell me I'm fat?' she demanded. 'What a cheek!'

He dodged the towel and said smoothly, 'Not at all—you look perfect to me. I don't go for stick insects...give me curves every time!'

Emma felt a flush of embarrassment colour her cheeks—these observations of his were a little too intimate. She turned to the sea and sprinted as quickly as she could towards the breaking waves, gasping as her legs hit the water and she felt the shock of its icy coldness.

'Wow,' she shrieked. 'It's *awful*—simply freezing!'

A spray of water landed on her body, making her shriek even more. She turned round and Sean was behind her, splashing water over her and laughing at her.

'Come on,' he shouted. 'It's not so bad—start swimming and you'll get used to it!'

'Stop it! How could you?' she shouted back. She dived away from him in desperation, working her arms and legs to try and get some warmth into them. In a minute he had caught up with her, his hair plastered wetly across his brow, brilliant blue eyes twinkling mischievously at her.

'I'll give you a ten-second start and race you to the black rock over there,' he said.

'And why should I need a ten-second start, for goodness' sake?' Emma enquired indignantly. 'We'll set off together...ready, steady, go!'

She set off in a mad crawl, arms whirling, gasping for air at every stroke, determined to get there before Sean, exerting every muscle to show him that she didn't need any favours when it came to races. When she looked up he was already there, a complacent grin on his face.

'You should have accepted my offer of a start,' he said smugly.

She flicked water over his face. 'I wasn't trying that time—just being kind to you.'

'Really? Well, I should thank you for that...and don't spray me again, young lady, or you won't get any smoked salmon.'

He caught her arm playfully and the swell of the waves pushed them together. Emma jolted against his naked chest, her bare legs brushing against his. It wasn't really a surprise when she felt as if hundreds of little electric shocks were darting through the lower regions of her stomach. Didn't that happen whenever Sean was near her? They stared at each other for a moment, his eyes holding hers with a burning look of desire. Suddenly his grip on her arm became firmer, and he pulled her against him. Her body felt boneless, unable to resist—and not wanting to either. Emma's head was spinning with the unexpectedness of it all—one minute they had been swimming together—the next she was entwined in his body. And the thing was, it felt too wonderful to stop.

But she hadn't wanted this, had she? Her thoughts were panicky, confused—every erogenous zone in her body screamed for him to continue, and yet good sense told her not to let things go too far. She'd allowed events to get out of hand with Mike once long ago, and then she'd been in his power, unable to break free until it had been too late...

Then Sean's hand drew her face to his, and his lips

covered her mouth in a salty, hard kiss that made her want to scream with a longing to give into him completely. When she felt his hands unhook her bikini top she did nothing to stop him but pressed herself against him harder, her soft breasts crushed against his hard body. She felt him shudder and he buried his face in her neck.

'Beautiful Emma,' he whispered. 'Can't we take these damn things off altogether...?'

And Emma felt her last reserves slipping away. What did it matter? she thought, ignoring the warning voices that whispered primly in her head that he was a colleague, and that she didn't want to get involved with a man again. Surely she'd been celibate for long enough now, paying for her guilt by denying herself for all these years. All at once she didn't care any more—she'd tried to tell Sean that she wasn't ready for commitment, warned him she was no good at relationships, and if he didn't care about that, then why should she? On this lovely summer's afternoon with the water lapping gently over her body, there seemed no reason on earth to deny herself any longer.

With a sense of abandonment she pulled at her bikini bottom and wriggled out of it, and then firmly and deliberately tugged at Sean's trunks until he kicked them off. He pulled her towards him and their bodies melted together, his hard and demanding, hers soft and yielding, and his kisses were hard and passionate, teasing her lips apart as they bobbed in the swell of the water.

'This is crazy,' she whispered, as his hands explored her body, caressing her full breasts and making little explosions of desire thrill every nerve. 'I didn't mean to do this at all...it was the last thing I wanted...'

He laughed softly. 'I don't believe you, sweetheart. I know...I can tell, that you want it as much as I do...' He pulled away from her for a second, his blue eyes suddenly serious, searching hers. 'But I'm not doing anything you'll regret. If you feel it's not right then stop me now, my love...'

She touched his lips with her fingers and whispered, 'Perhaps this is the point of no return.' Then she sighed. 'But this is for today. Who knows what will happen tomorrow. Perhaps by then I'll be sorry.'

A fleeting frown crossed his face, then he said fiercely, 'I promise you that won't happen. You'll always be glad that we did this on a hot sunny day whilst swimming in the sea together. How lovely is this?'

Emma wound her arms around his neck and parted her legs to his insistent body. Somehow the lapping of the water on their naked bodies increased their desire to fever pitch. They lost themselves in each other, and waves of sweetness swept through her as he shuddered with ecstasy, and she felt a joyful power at her ability to satisfy him.

Afterwards they clung to each other for several minutes, savouring the sweet aftermath of fulfilment, his arms clasped round her as they rocked in the water.

'That was...unbelievable,' Sean finally whispered in her ear. 'How was it for you, sweetheart?'

'Too wonderful.' Emma's smile was mischievous. 'But it's made me ravenously hungry and thirsty!'

He grinned. 'Well, let's go and have our picnic. I hope we haven't got too much of an audience when we run out of the sea—we seem to have lost our swimwear!'

They raced across the sand towards their clothes,

Emma giggling as the warm sun touched her naked body. This certainly hadn't been what she'd intended earlier in the day!

How good the wine tasted—slightly astringent, fresh and cold from the cool-bag. Emma sipped it languorously as she sat back on the rug, her back against a tree-trunk, shaded by the gnarled branches above them. She closed her eyes for a moment, trying to marshal her thoughts, which were whizzing crazily round her head like the shaken pieces in a kaleidoscope. It had been so wonderful…so passionate, the reality of making love to Sean everything she had been dreaming of…. And yet she felt a loss of power, the feeling that now Sean would be calling the shots, that now she'd be under his spell like she had been with Mike. Had she made one great big mistake this afternoon, allowed the passion of the moment to overtake good sense?

She sighed. Why did life have to be so damn complicated? Why couldn't she have made love to Sean and then forgotten all about it? How much simpler that would be, one afternoon of love without any of the drawbacks of falling madly in love with the man!

Sean watched her closely then, tracing a pattern in the sand with a stick, he said casually, 'Why the sigh, Emma? Regretting it already?'

She answered a little too quickly, 'No—no, of course not. It was fantastic, unbelievable… It's just that…'

He rolled over on his stomach and looked up at her grimly. 'It's just that you're still afraid, aren't you? Afraid you've given too much and whatever it was that happened with that other guy will happen with us?'

Emma stared out at the glinting sea. He was right—up to a point. His circumstances weren't the same as

Mike's, but nevertheless it was fear of a man's power over her that stopped her from giving herself completely.

'You still love him, don't you?' Sean's voice was hard, relentless. 'Even after this afternoon he's still in your heart, isn't he?'

'No! No, that's not true!' Emma almost spat the words out. 'I don't love Mike now—but I hate what I became when I was with him.'

Sean sat up and leaned towards her. 'What do you mean? Just what happened between you?'

She sighed. Was this the right time to tell Sean her sad little tale of a broken heart? She scooped up a handful of sand and watched the grains run through her fingers, looking at him under her lashes. His good opinion of her might change rather swiftly, she thought sadly, and what good anyway would it be to tell Sean about her turbulent love life. That was in the past.

She smiled at him and said as lightly as she could, 'Can't we just enjoy the moment, Sean? I don't regret anything of today...but, as I warned you before, I'm not into deep relationships yet.'

He was silent for a moment as if digesting her words, then he looked across at her with a sudden sweet smile. 'Yes,' he murmured, tracing her tanned arm with his finger. 'Why don't we live for today? I can handle that, if that's what you want. No strings attached, but plenty of fun.'

Emma nodded, but there was a fraction of doubt in her mind. How easy was it going to be to keep her feelings for Sean on a casual basis when she felt such a powerful sexual attraction for him whenever they met, and after what had happened that afternoon?

Sean watched Emma as she pulled her hair back into its ponytail. Yes—he could live with that, because he was absolutely sure that what had started lightly could become very serious indeed one day.

'So, how was your hot date?' Charles was pouring himself a drink in the sitting room when Emma came back. 'See any dolphins, or was it all a ploy to get his wicked way with you?'

Emma flushed. She still hadn't come down to earth from the events of the afternoon, her mind in a turmoil, one second on air when she remembered the wonder of Sean's love-making, the next second in nervous doubt that she had gone too far to retreat in her relationship with him.

Her brother didn't know how close to the truth he'd been, but he sure had the power to irritate her more than any man she knew, and the sooner she moved into her little cottage, the better! Then she bit her lip. Surely there couldn't be any foundation in what Charles had said about Sean's motives? Perhaps, she thought with dismay, it hadn't been an impulsive act of the moment, but all planned… Then she pushed the thought forcefully to the back of her mind, refusing to believe that Sean could be that calculating.

'I don't know what you mean, Charles,' she said loftily. 'Yes, we saw lots of dolphins, and they were absolutely wonderful, diving in and out of the water. The most amazing show, and I loved it.'

Charles looked at her sardonically. 'So it was purely a nature trip? Be careful, little sister, you may have had your thoughts only on dolphins but I bet your colleague didn't!'

Emma forced a smile on her face. 'Not everyone's like you, Charles! Now, tell me, did Ben enjoy the little fair?'

'He sure did.' Her brother grinned. 'Poor little thing's worn out now! He did everything—roundabouts, riding on a donkey, eating ice cream. He didn't want to come home!'

He drew a cigarette out of a silver cigarette box and lit it, inhaling deeply and blowing out the smoke then smiling in his engaging way at Emma. 'You wouldn't babysit for me tonight, would you? Mother's out and I've got to go and see someone rather urgently.'

'I'd be pleased to. Is he in bed now?'

'Yes. He should be no trouble.' Charles's eyes softened a little. 'He's a great little chap—we had a lot of fun this afternoon.'

Charles might have his faults, thought Emma, going upstairs to check on Ben, but he adores his little boy. She gazed down at Ben lying asleep in his little bed, his favourite teddy beside him and a smear of chocolate over his plump cheek. It would be lovely for her mother to have her grandson in the house and watch him playing in the garden like she and her brother had so many years ago, she reflected, and it was great for her also to have him so near. Next week she would take Ben to the beach outside her new home and have fun with him there and see how the builders were getting on with putting in the new windows. At least there would be no complicated relationships with this young male!

CHAPTER SIX

'WHAT the hell's going on in that waiting room—it sounds like a zoo!' Sean looked up irritably from his careful stitching of a man's cheek.

'A gang of drunks, I think,' said Bob Leeming grimly. He was involved in doing the same thing to another youth with a slashed hand. 'Just the usual happy party on a night-time jolly. I was always told by my mum that a night out was a time to relax and have fun. I don't think she meant this type of activity!'

Sean sighed. 'Have we called in Security? I'll go along myself and see what's happening now I've finished with Fred here.' He patted the arm of the patient he'd been dealing with. 'I don't want to see you in here again,' he said, then he turned and walked briskly down the corridor towards the noise.

Connie passed him at a trot and raised her eyes to heaven. 'Going to be one of those nights,' she said breathlessly. 'Got a young girl haemorrhaging in cubicle eight and every bed on the gynae ward is filled. I'm going to have to take Bob away from suturing that lad. I'll get Bill to finish off there.'

Sean nodded sombrely. It was a typical night shift with a shortage of staff and beds and far too many patients who had to be juggled around. There'd been a change-over in staff—Sean's team were working a 9 p.m. to 7 a.m. shift and it was going to be a very long ten hours, he reflected, opening the waiting-room doors to a rather familiar scene.

A gang of youths was bunched round the reception desk, shouting obscenities at Katie Marshall and demanding that their friend be seen immediately. One of them was standing on a chair and swinging his arms wildly, and a group of innocent onlookers was by the door, looking increasingly anxious as the situation spiralled.

In a corner Emma and Tania were bending over the prone body of an elderly homeless man who had collapsed on the floor. They were beckoning urgently to Zak to bring a trolley.

Sean swore under his breath and strode over to the knot of youths now cackling in drunken amusement at Katie's discomfort. She looked across at Sean with relief.

'I've pressed the emergency button,' she mouthed at him through the glass. 'The police should be here soon.'

The youth on the chair began hammering at the desk window. 'Come on, you old cow,' he yelled. 'Get someone to see my mate now. He's hurt his wrist and his nose…'

The lad gave a yelp as he felt himself lifted bodily out of the chair and deposited none too gently on the floor. 'Gerroff,' he screamed. 'Don't bloody touch me…'

Sean smiled grimly as he looked down at the infuriated lad. 'Please, don't stand on the chairs,' he said in a steely but pleasant voice, still holding the youth's arms in a vice-like grip. He looked round at the group of youths, silenced momentarily by this diversion and the intimidating authority in Sean's face. 'If you don't all go now,' he added with quiet menace, 'you'll be arrested by the police I can see coming through the doors.'

They looked belligerently at him, and one shaven-headed lout with an impressive amount of body piercing thrust his chin towards Sean.

'Don't tell us what we can do, or I'll—'

'You'll do what?'

Sean was a big man, towering above them, and the lout scowled mutinously but retreated, muttering vague threats, his eye on the three hefty policeman who were making their way purposefully in their direction.

'What about our mate?' said one of the youths sullenly. 'We could sue you for not looking after him.'

'He can stay. The rest of you—*out*!'

Sean left the long arm of the law to finish the job and went over to Emma and Tania, who were now administering oxygen to the scruffy old man lying on the ground.

'What's happened here?' Sean asked.

'It's Eli Shepperton,' said Tania. 'He's one of our regulars—comes in for some warmth and TLC every so often. The poor old man's passed out. He said his toe was very painful and it does look white.'

'It's cold and pulseless,' confirmed Emma. 'Looks like an acutely ischaemic toe, probably related to peripheral vascular disease.'

'Then let's get him through quickly and ring up the emergency vascular surgeon—they'll probably do an angioplasty to open up any blockage in the blood vessel,' said Sean. 'Zak and I will take his top half, Emma and Tania, you take his legs. One, two, three, up!'

Between them they heaved the limp old man onto the trolley and Eli was then pushed through to one of the cubicles.

'What on earth was going on at Reception?' asked Emma as they walked down the corridor.

Sean shrugged. 'Just an everyday story of life in Casualty. The local lads enjoying themselves on a night out.' He raised a hand in farewell as he swung off to another cubicle. 'See you soon. I'd better get back to the patient I was dealing with before I had the pleasure of meeting our friends in Reception! I'll ring through to get a team on standby for Eli first.'

'Thank heaven for Sean,' murmured Tania to Emma as they started to work on Eli when they got to the cubicle, cutting away his trouser legs and hooking him up to a monitor. 'Did you see the way he sorted out those yobbos?' She sighed theatrically. 'He's a treasure, that man. Real tough hero material, don't you think? And looks to die for as well! Why he hasn't been snapped up yet I can't imagine!'

'He's not bad-looking,' agreed Emma cautiously as she studied Eli's affected foot closely.

She wondered how Tania would react if she revealed that Sean and she were more than friendly colleagues—probably broadcast it on the hospital radio, she wouldn't wonder! Emma's pulse bounded into overdrive as a vivid picture flashed into her mind of Sean and herself making love in the sea together totally naked—a scenario as far removed from the one going on in Casualty as could be imagined! Had it only been two days ago that they'd been in the secluded little bay, just the two of them? And now they were in the middle of the noise and chaos of a busy emergency department, with no time even to look at each other or talk.

Eli stirred and groaned, his eyes fluttering open and looking in an unfocussed way at Emma and Tania.

'My foot,' he muttered. 'It hurts like hell.'

'It's all right, Eli,' said Emma soothingly. 'I can make that feel easier. I'm going to give you an injection of pethidine which should block the pain. Lie back and try and relax.'

Emma bent forward over the old man's arm, pinching the skin to try and find a vein before she gave him an injection and tried to concentrate on the matter in hand. But it was hard—the magic of that afternoon would stay with her for ever, and the thought of trying to maintain a professional distance after that almost laughable. Tania's voice interrupted her thoughts abruptly.

'BP OK, pulse 100, oxygen stats OK,' she intoned as she watched the monitor recording Eli's vital signs. 'There you are, Eli. Not too bad…'

The old man looked at her cynically. 'That's what they all say when you're dying,' he said darkly. 'What can they do about this foot of mine? I can't even walk to the pub at the moment!'

Emma put her hand on his arm reassuringly. He was putting on a show of bravado, like many patients, but she knew that he inside he was very frightened.

'You're not dying, Eli, but you need emergency treatment on that toe. We're getting through to the vascular surgeon now and hopefully he can get the circulation going again. When did it start getting painful?'

'Last night, just as I was settling down with me

mates. I'd just had a couple of drinks and, bingo! I thought my foot was going to come off!'

'Only a couple of drinks, Eli?' said Tania, mock-sternly. 'You promised us last time you were in that you'd keep off the meths!'

Eli chuckled, cheered slightly by Emma's reassurance and Tania's teasing. 'It wasn't meths,' he growled, 'Just a nice light chilled wine.' He winked at them both, then said plaintively, 'Don't bully me, Nurse. I need some strong hot tea now. Have you got any?'

'I'm afraid we can't give you anything by mouth at the moment because I hope you'll be going into Theatre very soon.'

'Then let me have a smoke—you can't deny me that surely?'

'Sorry, Eli, it's a non-smoking hospital anyway. You'll have to hang on for a while. Besides, you know it's bad for you.'

'Sadists,' muttered Eli. 'No drink, no smokes, no women—life's not worth living!' He lay back on the pillow and closed his eyes.

'I'll just go and see if Dr Casey managed to get hold of the surgeon,' Emma said to Tania.

She swung off through the curtains of the cubicle and almost collided with Sean coming in.

'Ah, Dr Fulford,' he murmured, catching her arm and smiling down at her. 'Just the person I wanted to see. Mr Vernon is coming down to see Eli Shepperton and assess his condition, and they're ready to take him to Theatre.'

'Good—I've given him 50 milligrams of pethidine

for his pain and his obs seem reasonable in the circumstances.'

Sean still held her arm. He pulled her slightly nearer to him.

'I wanted to talk to you, but it's been rather a hell of a night and I haven't had a chance.'

'You're right,' said Emma, the familiar fluttering in her stomach starting over again at his touch. 'It's like a madhouse here at the moment...'

She pulled her arm gently from his grasp—physical contact with Sean at work didn't do her concentration any good at all. She tried to move round him, but he put one of his arms up against the wall, blocking her way and looking down at her intently.

'Just give me a few seconds. I see the builders have started at your cottage. When are you going to move in?'

'I'm going to look at the place this weekend—bringing my little nephew with me. If the builders have got on fairly well I may move in a fortnight—by which time we'll be working days again, thank heavens. I've never been very good on nights.'

Sean chuckled. 'Emma, honey, I just don't believe that—but I'd like to find out if it's true...'

Emma giggled, then said reprovingly, 'Sean Casey, remember what we agreed—nothing too heavy!'

He raised his eyebrows. 'Of course! Just a light romance with no strings...' Then his expression changed as he looked down at her. 'Nevertheless, I can't wait for us to be together again. A week's going to be an eternity—especially after what happened the last time we were together. I can't get it out of mind,' he added softly.

He tilted her face towards his and his mouth hovered dangerously near hers, sending her pulse into overdrive.

Emma looked guiltily around. 'For heaven's sake, Sean, someone will see us. I'm supposed to be ministering to the sick, and so are you, not…well, not doing this!'

His eyes opened wide in innocent surprise. 'So someone sees us. I'm only examining your eyes, making medically certain that the irises really are this special shade of velvety brown. It must be most unusual.'

Emma laughed and pushed him firmly away from her, and a loud grumbling voice came from the cubicle behind them.

'When's that doctor going to let me have a smoke? All this tosh about it being a non-smoking hospital—that's just an excuse to deny a poor old man his human rights!'

'Looks like you're in demand from everyone,' remarked Sean with a grin. 'Remember I've booked you for next Saturday—and I'd like to meet your nephew!'

As Emma turned back towards the cubicle to tell Eli the surgeon was coming to see him, she suddenly felt a wave of happiness ripple through her. All at once life seemed more positive, full of a promise she hadn't felt for years.

Maybe Sean and she were only living for the moment, but perhaps she was gradually coming to terms with her past and putting it behind her.

She put a hand on the curtain to pull it back when a voice from behind hailed her loudly.

'Emma! Emma! Can I see you for a minute?'

She turned in surprise and saw a familiar figure

walking through the doors from the waiting room. It was her brother—the last person she expected to see in Casualty!

'What are you doing here?' she demanded anxiously. 'Is there something wrong? Have you had an accident?'

'No…no, I'm fine. Just wanted a quick word with you.'

'Is it about Mum—has something happened to her?'

'Keep your hair on, sis!' said Charles with his charming smile. 'No—nothing to be worried about. As I said, I just needed to see you for a minute. The receptionist said I could come through.'

Emma sighed—a mixture of relief and slight foreboding, for she felt sure that Charles wouldn't come to the hospital on just a whim.

'Come into the kitchen, then, but make it snappy! Well, what is it?'

Her brother stood in front of her and shuffled his shoes rather uncomfortably. 'It's a bit awkward,' he began, 'but I've something to ask you…'

No surprise there, thought Emma wryly, bracing herself for the request. 'Well?' she said impatiently. 'Be quick!'

'The thing is…I'm afraid I've got myself into a bit of a pickle—only temporarily, of course…'

Emma went slightly cold. 'What kind of a pickle, Charles?'

'A bit of debt actually, more a cash-flow problem than anything else. I wondered if you could sub me for a short while…'

'How much debt, for heaven's sake?'

'Don't lose your rag, Emma—just two thousand. Once it's cleared, I'll be all right.'

'*What?* Two thousand pounds? You must be mad. You know I'm buying this cottage—what makes you think I've got that much to spare?'

Emma looked in shocked amazement at her brother and he grinned rather shamefacedly, but said defiantly enough, 'I don't want to bother Mother about it...'

'I should think not,' retorted Emma hotly. 'She's only just been widowed, she's trying to start a new business—the last thing she needs to know is that you're in debt!'

There was a hint of warning in his voice. 'That's why she mustn't know—but if I leave it much longer she's bound to find out. Moneylenders have a way of exacting their dues, you know!'

'You're blackmailing me, Charles. You mean that if I don't cough up, you'll ask Mother?'

'It's not blackmail,' Charles said reasonably. 'It's just that it would be a better way...can't you see that?'

Emma was silent. She had the money from the small nest egg she'd saved over the years—she didn't want her brother to be in danger, as he'd implied, neither did she want her mother worrying over her brother's indiscretions.

At last she said reluctantly, 'I'll see what I can do—but I must know, Charles, where the hell has the money gone?'

For the first time Charles looked truly embarrassed. 'I, er, had a few little flutters on the horses, but I picked the wrong ones. I was trying to raise some cash quickly. I won at first, then things started to go pear-shaped.'

'You gambled it away?'

'Don't worry, I'll get it back.'

'If I give you this money, Charles, you'll darn well pay me back, every penny. I work hard for my money—don't you dare squander it on horses again.' She pointed to the door. 'And now get out before anyone sees you...I'm supposed to be on duty!'

She watched her brother saunter back to Reception, looking as if he hadn't a care in the world. How could he allow himself to run up such debts? She turned away in annoyance and marched towards the cubicles, passing Sean on the way. He looked quizzically at Charles's disappearing figure and then at her cross face.

'Awkward customer?' he asked.

'You could say that,' she replied, tight-lipped. 'But I've dealt with him!'

It was a week later and a blustery Saturday afternoon. Emma drew in large gulps of the salty refreshing air blowing from the sea and gave a silent cheer of joy that her stint on nights had ended. She couldn't wait to see how the builders were getting on with the alterations and repairs to the cottage. Then perhaps she could make arrangements for the move.

Ben held Emma's hand tightly and looked at the little cottage facing them.

'Is this where you're going to live?' he asked.

'Yes—it's got to have a lot of things put right first, but then I'll move in. What do you think of it?'

The little boy inspected the cottage solemnly, his head on one side.

'I like it,' he pronounced finally. 'It looks like the Three Bears' House. Has it got a bedroom?'

Emma laughed. 'It's got two bedrooms—you can

come and stay in one of them when the builders have moved out.'

Builders' ladders and rubble still lay on the ground, but the windows and front door had been replaced and a new wash of light pink had been applied to the plaster exterior—the place was beginning to look well cared-for again.

Ben seized Emma's hand again, bored with inspecting her new property. 'Let's dig some sandcastles and big holes for the water,' he begged, tugging her towards the beach. As if promising her a reward afterwards, he added, 'We can come back here after we've done some digging.'

He scampered over the sand to where he'd left his bucket and spade and started immediately, his little figure bent industriously over his spade, sand flying out behind him as he dug a small trench to the sea. Then he seized his bucket and trotted down to the water to fill it, then poured the contents into the hole he'd dug. He watched it drain away in dismay and looked up sadly at Emma.

'The water's all gone,' he said mournfully. 'You get some for me!'

Emma dropped a kiss on his round little face and went to refill the bucket. When she came back Sean had arrived and was bending down by Ben and helping him build a sandcastle, using his hands to dig out the sand.

'You've got your work cut out.' She smiled. 'Ben has very exacting standards.'

Sean straightened up. He was looking rugged in a thick jersey and jeans and she almost had to stop herself rushing into his arms. His smile was slow and intimate, almost as if he knew what she was thinking, his glance raking her figure hungrily.

'Good to see you, Emma.'

They stared at each other for a second, oblivious to their surroundings, then Sean looked down at Ben as if realising suddenly where he was.

'I've introduced myself already to this young man,' said Sean. 'He's a hard taskmaster—got me working straight away!'

Ben looked at them both seriously with big brown eyes. 'We've got to be quick,' he informed them. 'Emma says the sea will come in soon.' He frowned for a moment. 'Will it go out again?'

Sean laughed. 'Yes, it will, Ben, but by then it will have knocked over your castle so we've not got a lot of time to build it.'

Ben nodded happily. 'It'll be the biggest castle in the whole world—then we can all have an ice cream!'

'I look forward to that,' said Sean gravely.

Emma watched the two of them—large man and very small boy, working together energetically. Ben was filled with excited enthusiasm, occasionally running round to see what Sean was doing, and just like a little foreman telling him what he wanted done! Occasionally Sean looked up and winked at Emma.

'I thought I'd be having a rest this weekend,' he commented.

'You'd make a great father,' Emma replied, grinning at him.

He flipped his dark hair back with one hand and laughed, his eyes holding hers and dancing with humour. 'Now, that's a thought,' he said. 'I've always wanted a large family...how about you?'

'I haven't thought about it much,' Emma lied.

For, of course, she'd thought about having children, wondering as the years went by if she'd ever meet anyone she'd like to have children with. And now she was embarrassed to have raised a subject that was far too intimate for two people to discuss who were only having a fun relationship—which, of course, she and Sean were…

She looked at Sean kneeling down and patting the sand over the castle they'd made, his hair tousled over his tanned face, and it came to her quite suddenly with the force of a thunderbolt that it was all so simple really—the man she was looking for to be the father of her children was right in front of her!

Perhaps she'd been blind before, too worried about making another mistake, but wasn't Sean everything she wanted in a man? She hadn't thought so at first—he'd seemed arrogant and overbearing, but now, watching the way he related to little Ben, the way he dealt with his patients, she was sure that the attraction she felt for Sean wasn't merely physical. She'd fallen for the whole person—kindly, compassionate and fun! She knew now that she had finally laid the ghost of Mike and the hold he had had over her.

'Emma Fulford,' she whispered to herself, 'I think you've found what you were looking for at last…'

Then a spattering of rain hit her face. The day had clouded over, the sky threatening squalls to come. It was time to go.

'We'd better get back to the cottage before we're soaked,' she said. 'I want to see how the alterations inside are going.'

Ben ran up to her, his eyes shining. 'Look at the

castle Sean and me made!' he shouted. 'Make him come tomorrow and we can do another one!'

Emma took his hand and they ran towards the cottage with Sean following. 'Sean may be busy tomorrow—he can't come every day,' she replied, opening the front door of the cottage.

'Yes, he can! He told me that if you were here he'd come willy-nilly. What does willy-nilly mean?'

'It means, young man,' explained Sean coming up behind them, 'that I'll do whatever Emma wants me to do…and I meant that,' he added softly.

Ben looked at them both and said triumphantly, 'See? He'll come if you say!'

They both laughed, then Sean looked round the little sitting room and made a wry face. 'Doesn't look as if you'll be in next week, Emma,' he said. 'Have they started on the kitchen yet?'

'Yes, but it's a bit chaotic,' admitted Emma. 'Anyway, I've made up my mind—I'm going to move next week whether it's ready or not. I love my brother but if we're under the same roof for much longer, I think we'll come to blows!'

She bit her lip. She hadn't meant to mention Charles, but since he had asked her for the money she was noticing more and more that, although he owed so much, he was certainly not cutting down on his spending. In the past week he'd come back with a new suit and he seemed to be out every evening meeting friends and, she had no doubt, having expensive meals. It made her uneasy to feel that their mother was ignorant of Charles's debts—and just how much could he be trusted to help Mrs Fulford in her new business venture?

'He lives with you and your mother, then?'

'Yes, he's going to help my mother with the bed and breakfast business she's starting. Sadly, his wife left him so little Ben lives with us too—which, of course, we love.'

Emma wondered suddenly if Annette had left Charles because he'd been gambling. They had always seemed to be short of money, and she had not been the type of woman to try and economise. Charles had always had plenty of charm, but there was no doubt about it—he was an unreliable pain to live with!

Sean looked at her perceptively. 'I imagine you're very different, you and your brother?'

'You can say that again. To be fair, my father gave Charles a hard time when he was young. My brother was never an academic, and had no interest at all in medicine.'

'And Professor Fulford was disappointed?'

'I'll say. He forced Charles to do his A levels, and when my brother failed them, my father washed his hands of him. I'm afraid Charles has rather drifted since then.'

Sean didn't comment, but he reflected ruefully that Professor Fulford sounded as if his unsympathetic attitude had affected his son's life adversely. He thought of his own family, once very happy, also damaged by the professor—indeed, his father would never be the same man again. Then Sean looked across at Emma, patiently helping Ben to sort out some seashells they'd found, her dark coppery hair falling in tendrils over her shoulders. He couldn't blame Emma for her father's actions and now he loved her, dammit, whatever her father had done!

'Why don't we all go and get that ice cream you talked about, Ben?' he asked cheerily. 'I know I've deserved it!'

Ben looked up with a happy beam. 'That's a good idea—come on, everybody!'

He scrambled to his feet and took both their hands, dragging Emma and Sean towards the door.

Emma laughed. 'Looks like we've got no option—he's a very masterful little boy!'

'Then I'd say he takes after his aunty,' murmured Sean, his eyes twinkling. 'And I can't wait for her to move next door, however bossy she is!'

Emma pulled a wry face at him, then murmured, 'I can't wait to move either!'

CHAPTER SEVEN

THE first night in her new little house! Emma snuggled down in her bed with a feeling of satisfaction and content. It was quite a wild night, and she could hear the breakers pounding on the shore and the wind howling round the cottage—but it felt warm and cosy inside, and at last she was independent. She adored her mother, but she was sure it was the best thing to move out of the house and away from Charles and the possibility that he would make further demands on her. She smiled to herself in the darkness—wasn't it an added bonus that she would be so near Sean?

It had been a mad day, moving her possessions out of her mother's house, taking delivery of the few bits of furniture she'd bought and cleaning up after the mess the builders had made. She was totally exhausted. Sean had arrived with a bottle of champagne and some very practical help, putting up cupboards and pictures and bringing a Chinese take-away round at the end of the day. She would be eternally grateful to him for that.

Tomorrow, she thought sleepily, she would put everything in the right cupboards, tidy up the little garden and plan what plants she would put there. She began to drift off to sleep…

The telephone rang harshly in her ear, its strident tones cutting abruptly into a lovely dream where she and Sean were walking over the downs on a hot day.

She sat up dazedly and held the phone to her ear, sure that it was some disaster that had befallen her mother.

'Emma? Sorry to wake you up.'

'Sean! What is it?'

'An emergency, I'm afraid.' His voice was clipped, terse. 'There's a red alert at the hospital and they need a team to go to a building that's collapsed in a gas explosion. Connie needs all the staff she can get in Casualty, so I could do with your help.'

'Of course,' she said wearily. She could hardly refuse. She knew he wouldn't have woken her unless it was something dire—and, after all, it was part of the job she'd trained for.

'Good. I'll pick you up in three minutes. We'll meet the paramedics on site.'

He rang off, and Emma looked at the phone in her hand as if it had just played a trick on her.

'Oh, hell,' she groaned. 'Can I really force myself to get dressed?'

She crawled out of bed and grabbed the warmest things she could find. It might be summer but tonight the weather was fierce, and they could be outside for a long time.

Sean was waiting for her on the road above the cottage. Emma glanced over at the sea before she got in the car. The rollers were crashing onto the shore, the boiling foam white in the dark night. The sea wasn't all that far from her little garden wall—she hoped the tide was on the turn.

'You're a star,' said Sean. 'You must be exhausted, but we need everyone we can get.'

'What's happened?' asked Emma, clipping on her seat belt as Sean accelerated down the road.

'Not too sure of the details, but it's thought a couple of squatters in one of the run-down buildings at the back of Carrfield tried to run a makeshift pipe from the mains gas to a stove. The explosion that happened later has brought down most of the building and destabilised the houses on either side. The young couple are both trapped and some people have been injured by falling masonry.'

'It sounds bad. I take it the other services are there?'

'They are, and I think we can see them now...'

Down the hill blue lights were flashing from the emergency vehicles and a small crowd had gathered, hunched figures staring in horror at the scene. As they got nearer, Emma could see the devastation the explosion had caused.

'It looks as though a bomb's fallen on the place,' she whispered. 'How can anyone be alive in that?'

'We'll soon find out,' muttered Sean, skidding to a halt and parking the car near the bystanders. 'Here,' he said, throwing a bundle to Emma. 'Put those on—a helmet and a coat to identify you.'

She put them on quickly, the fluorescent stripes on the coat had the word DOCTOR written in large capitals on the back. A paramedic came up to them, his face eerily white in the light of the arc lamps set up to illuminate the scene.

'Hello, Dr Casey, glad to see you. Most of the injured have been taken to Carrfield General, but we've got two victims both trapped under a beam, fairly close together. The firefighters are trying to move the beam, but we're concerned about the state of the young woman—apparently she's eight months pregnant and we think she's in labour.'

Sean seized his medical bag and said tersely, 'Let's go, then—OK, Emma?'

Both victims were lying under a heap of rubble out of which a large piece of wood protruded. The man was conscious and trapped from the waist down, but the woman had her eyes closed, although they fluttered open occasionally and at times she gave a low moan. They were both young.

'This is Steve,' said the paramedic, squatting down beside the man and talking to him gently. 'It's all right, mate, these are the doctors. We want them to assess your condition—keep calm.' He turned to Emma and Sean and said quietly, 'Steve's BP's low—eighty over fifty—and I think his right leg's broken. He says it's agonising. Apparently the firefighters are worried his leg may be impaled under all this stuff—that's why they're taking it slowly.'

'No wonder he's in shock,' said Sean grimly.

Emma flicked a look at the man's pallid, sweating face. 'What do you think, Sean? Ten mils intravenous morphine?'

'Yes—and if you can get an IV line of Haemaccel in, that would help.'

Emma patted Steve's arm reassuringly. 'Don't worry, Steve, this will help ease the pain very quickly.'

Could the evening get much worse? wondered Emma as she injected the young man's arm. The rain had turned to hard pellets of hail and in the distance a rumble of thunder could be heard. Was it really only half an hour ago that I was tucked up in my cosy bed, warm and dry? she reflected wryly as she took in the devastating scene before her.

Sean glanced up at the ruined building, the rooms

exposed cruelly to the elements. Doors were hanging off their hinges on the upper storeys, torn wallpaper flapping from the collapsed walls, and there was an ominous creaking noise. A fireman came up to them, his face grimed with dust.

'Better get a move on—we're worried about the state of the walls. We want to move the beam, but it's going to be a difficult operation without disturbing all that rubble and bringing it down on the young couple. I think we have the best chance of moving the young lady first—her name's Amy.'

'Help her,' croaked Steve desperately. 'She's started to have the baby—that's why I tried to link up the gas supply. She was getting cold and I wanted to make a hot drink for her.'

'And do you know how often she was getting contractions?' asked Emma, kneeling down by the couple. 'Were they very strong?'

'Yeah, she was in a lot of pain. About every five minutes, I reckon...' His voice sank to a despairing whisper. 'It's all my fault. Will she be OK?'

'Don't worry—we'll get her out,' said Emma crisply, giving the familiar reassuring words an upbeat inflexion but privately gulping with horror at the closeness of the contractions.

She took a pack of Haemaccel from Sean's bag. and looked up at him. 'I'll give Amy some fluids through an IV line—try and reduce the shock.'

'Good. How's her BP?' asked Sean.

The paramedic watching the dial on the oximeter frowned. 'BP's raised, oxygen stats on the low side.'

The girl's eyes fluttered open and she looked in terror at the scene round her for a second, then her voice rose hysterically. 'Get me out! Get me out! I can't have the baby here...please!'

Sean took her hand and squeezed it. 'Come on, Amy, pecker up! I'm Dr Casey and this is Dr Fulford. Now, tell me—apart from your contractions, are you in any pain? Can you feel your legs and is there anything lying hard across your stomach?'

'No...no. I'm wedged in, but it doesn't hurt. I think I'm still sitting on the chair I was on when the explosion happened.'

The medics around her looked at each other in relief and Sean said reassuringly, 'It's your first baby. They usually take their time coming, so try and relax while they move this rubble from you.'

I hope he's right, thought Emma, a shiver of anxiety running through her like cold water. She knelt by the frightened girl and said comfortingly, 'Take deep breaths slowly...that would be good for your baby and you. The firemen have to take great care as they move this stuff, so be patient. There's lots of people helping, all determined to get you out.'

It was amazing, thought Sean, watching Emma talking soothingly to Amy, what the power of physical contact and a firm, kind voice could do to calm down a terrified victim. Amy's frightened voice became lower, more controlled, and she even managed a weak smile at her boyfriend.

'Take me out for a drink after all this is over, Steve,' she whispered.

Sean kept hold of the young girl's hand as the firemen began painstakingly lifting the rubble from the two victims, trying not to dislodge a small hill of debris just above them. They shouted instructions to each other, their voices whipped away by the strong wind.

'Is it safe to give Amy and Steve some oxygen?' asked Emma of the burly chief fire officer directing the operations. 'They're in shock and it would help their breathing.'

'Give us a few minutes, Doc. We may need to use an oxyacetylene torch here to get through some masonry—don't want the whole lot to explode.'

Amy suddenly gave a loud scream of pain and the small crowd of rescuers looked apprehensively towards her.

'Was that a contraction, love?' asked Sean gently. 'Grip my hand when you feel another one coming on.'

'Yes!' gasped Amy. 'Tell them to hurry—I can't last much longer.'

Steve turned his head towards her, his voice barely audible. 'Hang on, Amy, they're getting you out...'

The minutes ticked by with agonising slowness, and Amy's contractions were increasing in intensity.

'Only three minutes between the last two,' muttered Sean to Emma. 'Ask those men to hurry up, will you?'

One of the firemen heard Sean and nodded to him. 'I think we've cleared enough to get a sling round that beam now—it shouldn't take long to raise it.'

Slowly and carefully the beam was winched away from the victims and a small cheer went up from the onlookers.

'Thank God,' whispered Emma, as the paramedics rushed forward and gently lifted Amy's swollen figure from the debris and onto a stretcher. Amy was loaded into the first ambulance which sped away quickly up the hill with a police escort, its blue light flashing.

The two doctors turned their attention to Steve, still trapped by his legs. The paramedics had been talking to him all the time, diverting his attention from what was going on and keeping him as calm as possible.

'Get ready to splint his leg when they've moved all this stuff,' instructed Sean. 'He'll need a spinal board, of course.'

There was a shout of warning, and a fireman lifted Emma bodily out of the way of a wall which was buckling and falling in a crash of dust and noise beside them. She held her breath, terrified that Sean and Steve had both been buried in the new collapse.

For a few seconds all that could be heard was the wind howling and the rain hitting the pavement, then Sean's irritable voice floated over to the knot of firemen and medics waiting at the side.

'For God's sake, are you going to get Steve out or what? I don't want to spend the rest of the night here!'

It took another ten minutes to extricate Steve from the rubble, the team taking extreme care as they removed the twisted metal and concrete that trapped him. In the dark of the night the squeal of metal on metal sounded eerie and Emma talked to him continually until he was lifted gently out. A collar brace was put round his neck by a paramedic and then he was strapped to a spinal board.

'We don't know what other injuries Steve's sustained,' warned Sean. 'He's been subjected to severe crushing. Warn the trauma unit that he'll need full X-rays of his pelvis, tibia and fibia, of course. What do you think about his leg, Emma?'

Emma bent over and examined the torn bloody limb carefully. 'I can't see any protrusion of bone so it's probably not a compound break. Could be a comminuted fracture—that's quite likely with the amount of force he's suffered on that leg.'

'What will they do?' muttered Steve through dry lips. 'Take off my leg?'

Sean smiled at him. 'They won't do that—but I don't think you'll be playing football for a while.'

As he was borne off to the ambulance the young man whispered, 'Thanks…thanks for getting Amy out.'

They watched as the ambulance drove off and the little crowd of onlookers began to drift away. The firemen were erecting a fence around the damaged property.

Sean puffed out his cheeks with relief, then turned to Emma and put his arms round her. 'Are you frozen?' he asked.

'No—just absolutely exhausted, but so glad they were rescued. I'll have to go and see what happened to Amy tomorrow. I just hope the baby arrives OK.'

'Come on, then, let's get you back. I guess we could both do with a hot drink.'

They collapsed into Sean's car and were soon back at Emma's. Sean came down the path to the cottage with her and then they both stopped and stared in front of them in disbelief.

'What…what on earth's happened?'

Emma swallowed, trying hard to take in the scene she was looking at. The whole garden had been swept away, the little retaining wall had crumbled and sea water was swilling round the front door.

'I can't bear it,' she whispered, clutching Sean's arm. 'Look what the sea's done to my lovely little cottage.'

'Stay here,' he commanded, and started wading through the debris and sea water. 'I'll see what's happened inside.'

He unlocked the front door and pushed it open, turning on the light to see the damage. When he came back, Emma could see by his expression that all was not well.

'A bit of a mess, I'm afraid. It's not fit to go into tonight,' he reported. 'But don't worry,' he added quickly. 'We'll get it sorted—but not now!'

'You warned me about flooding,' she said mournfully. 'How could it happen tonight—my first night in the place?'

Sean looked at Emma's doleful face and put his arm round her. 'Sweetheart, it's not the end of the world, but right now we've had a hell of a night and there's only one place you're going to sleep and that's with me!'

Emma shook her head. 'I...I can't, Sean. It wouldn't be right!'

'Look, the only other bed I have is a damned uncomfortable sofa—and having spent most of the night rescuing people in a storm I don't fancy either of us using it.' His tired eyes danced at her for a second. 'We may not get much sleep anyway, but at least we'll enjoy it if we're together!'

'Oh, don't you see, Sean?' said Emma tiredly. 'It would be going past the point of no return. Once I've slept in your bed it makes it sort of permanent—more serious...'

Sean looked at her with a mixture of amusement and exasperation. 'For heaven's sake, girl, so what? We've already crossed the Rubicon and made love. And as for making it more permanent and serious...' He tilted her begrimed face to his and said softly, 'Would that really be so terrible?'

But I might get hurt again, Emma thought.

'You're still living in the past, my love—frightened of any commitment,' he added, as if reading her mind. 'Why don't you take a chance? If it's too horrible, you need never do it again!'

Emma laughed at his unexpected use of words and her tension suddenly evaporated. 'Of course I don't think it will be horrible—far from it! OK, I'm too tired to argue now...show me the way!'

They had a drink of cocoa laced with a tot of whisky and with a twinkle Sean tossed Emma a pair of his pyjamas.

'Not that I want you to wear them,' he murmured, 'but you could start off in them!'

After a quick shower, Emma fell into the bed, almost too tired to care where she was sleeping. She barely noticed when Sean slipped in beside her. He looked down at her exhausted face and smiled, kissing the corner of her mouth gently, then he pulled her close to him and curled round her soft body. They had plenty of time.

The bright morning sun poured through the edge of the curtains and warmed Emma's face. She opened her eyes sleepily and then suddenly was wide awake, feeling the weight and warmth of Sean's body wrapped round hers. The events of last night came rushing back to her—the drama of the rescue and the sinking feeling when she'd seen the damage to the cottage. And now, she thought in amazed wonder, here I am in Sean's bed! How far they'd come since the day they'd first met in the taxi and she'd vowed she'd never wanted to see him again or have anything to do with him!

She lay contentedly in his arms for a minute, savouring his closeness, then she twisted round and studied his face, so very close to hers. She could see the dark morning stubble on his chin and the long black lashes fringing his eyes. His hair was thick and rumpled over his forehead, and in sleep he had a boyish look about him that made him look rather defenceless and vulnerable. Why on earth, she wondered, had she even thought twice about his invitation to sleep in his bed with her?

She touched his eyebrow softly and drew her finger lightly over its arch and Sean's eyes opened suddenly, blue irises flecked with green looking deep into hers.

'Hello, sweetheart,' he said drowsily, then he grew more awake and grinned at her. 'Come here and let me say good morning to you!'

He drew her head towards his and kissed her gently on her lips, then his hands wandered over her body, peeling off the pyjamas, which were far too big for her anyway.

'Is this the way you say good morning?' asked Emma with a giggle.

'When you're with me, it is,' he said firmly. He squinted at the clock by the bed and chuckled. 'We've got half an hour before we need get up—so let's make the most of it!'

He started to kiss her with passionate intensity, his mouth bruising hers, teasing open her lips, then moving his lips down her neck and over her breasts with light kisses. She luxuriated in feeling his hard body over hers, arching her back in pleasure as his mouth fluttered over her stomach, revelling in the feel of his warm skin.

He pulled back the sheet and gazed down at Emma's slender but curvaceous body, with her narrow waist and full breasts, dappled by the light and shade in the room. She smiled up at him.

'I'm going to get cold with nothing on,' she whispered.

'Don't worry—I'll think of something to warm us up…' he said huskily. 'You are so beautiful, my darling Emma. The sexiest girl on earth…'

Then his hands moved gently over her body, exploring her most secret crevasses with gentle and expert insistence until she squirmed with desire and pleasure, all restraint gone.

'My God,' he breathed as he kissed her stomach. 'How soft your skin is—like satin.'

He buried his face in her soft breasts, and she felt his body hard and tense against hers, gently but firmly pressing her legs apart, and she longed for him to take her completely. And when he did it was wild and wonderful, making her whole body tremble. And finally he held her tenderly in his arms as they lay back in the aftermath of love.

'How wonderful was that, my sweet?' he whispered to her. 'What a way to start the day!'

Emma stirred in Sean's arms and sighed, twining his crisp hair round her fingers. 'Pity we've got to be in Casualty in half an hour!' Then she looked at him impishly. 'I hope you've got the stamina for a day's work after all that!'

'I don't know what you mean,' he said with a grin. He pulled her towards him and started to kiss her face once more. 'I could make love to you all day long. Let's start again, shall we?'

He gave a yell as a giggling Emma pushed him away. 'We haven't time...and anyway I'm starving. Is there anything in your fridge to eat?'

'Don't worry, I'm good at breakfasts.' He looked down at her lovingly for a second, his finger tracing the line of her jaw down to her neck. 'Are you glad you stayed the night, Emma? No regrets?'

She smiled back at him, her face alight with happiness. 'No regrets...none at all. It was blissful.'

'And you would tell me if there were?' he persisted. 'You must be honest with me.'

'Yes,' she replied firmly. 'There should be no secrets. I've had enough of that before.'

'Then you must stay here until your cottage is put right.' He looked down at with a grin, and added, 'Unless you want to put it on the market again. After all, we only need one place between us!'

She laughed. 'I thought we weren't into future commitment,' she teased.

'I think we've gone further than that, don't you?' he asked with a tender smile, bending his face to hers and kissing her gently on her lips.

A short time later Emma sat outside on the little terrace having steaming coffee and hot croissants in the warm sun. The storms of the night before had vanished and now the sky was clear, the sea a shimmering, glinting sheet of blue. She leaned back contentedly in her chair and looked down to the beach where Sean was throwing sticks for the dog before he set off for work. She had never felt happier. She was sure now that her future lay with Sean, that she could trust him and that he would never betray her like Mike had done. This time there would be no relationship built on lies—only honesty and truth.

All that day Emma was on cloud nine, so much so that Tania looked at her suspiciously.

'I don't know what you're on, Emma Fulford, but I'd like to get some of it! You've been on a high all day. I thought after the dreadful accident you attended last night you'd be exhausted!'

Emma seized gratefully on the accident to divert attention from her high spirits. 'I am exhausted,' she protested. 'I was there practically all night—I'll probably collapse later. And that's reminded me, I must go to Maternity and find out if Amy, one of the victims, has had her baby yet. She nearly gave birth while she was still trapped, and it was very scary, I can tell you.'

'I'll come with you,' said Sean behind her, making Emma's pulse rate bound into overdrive. 'I'd like to know what she had and if they're OK. We may as well go now as we're quite quiet.'

'Let's get some flowers from the hospital shop on the way.'

Amy was in a side ward, a small cot by her bed. She looked up as Emma and Sean came in and a little smile of recognition crossed her pale tired face.

'We came to see how you were after last night,' explained Emma. 'And, of course, we wanted to know what you had!'

'I had a little girl—I'm going to call her Britney

Emma,' said Amy shyly. 'I shan't forget how you helped last night—it's a kind of thank you.'

'I'm very flattered,' said Emma with a huge smile. 'I hope it brings her good luck!'

She peeped into the cot at the tiny baby with a crown of fluffy fair hair on her head. 'She's absolutely lovely, Amy—what a little treasure! You're a clever girl! May I cuddle her for a minute?'

'Of course you can—I've got to feed her again soon. She seems to need a lot of feeding!'

Emma took the baby in her arms and looked down at the peaceful little face, rosy pink, and gently touched the child's cheek. One day perhaps she'd have her own baby to hold—and it didn't seem such an outlandish dream any more, she reflected, flicking a quick glance towards Sean.

Sean laid the flowers they'd bought on the bed. 'I'm afraid these are all the hospital shop had to offer, but we didn't have time to get into Carrfield.' He looked at Amy solicitously, noting her dark-ringed eyes and pallor. 'Have you had any sleep since you gave birth?' he asked.

'Not much yet. They say I'm anaemic, and when I've had a blood transfusion I'll feel better.'

'And have you heard how Steve is?'

Amy shook her head. 'They told me he's broken his leg and his back's bad, but I don't know when they're letting him out. They're going to wheel me round to see him soon.'

'And where will you all go—you can't go back to the squat, can you?' asked Sean gently.

'My mum says she'll have us…' Amy plucked at the sheet on her bed and suddenly looked rather distressed.

'We shouldn't have done what we did with the gas pipe—I'm sorry some other people got injured.'

Two big tears rolled down her cheeks and Sean took her hand and said kindly, 'Don't think about that now. The main thing is that you're all right. You were very brave, Amy—it was terrifying for you being in labour and trapped under all that stuff. Thank God it all turned out well.'

'Yes,' said Amy in a small voice. 'I suppose you're right.'

As they walked back along the corridor together, Emma said, 'If you really mean what you say about my staying with you, what about dinner tonight? I'll do supper for us. Would lasagne and salad be OK?'

'Of course I meant what I said. You're staying with me until the cottage has been put to rights—or longer if possible! As for dinner, I'd love that, but I have to go out tonight and see my father.'

'Fine…but why don't you bring him over to us and I'll cook for us all? I'd love to meet him.'

Sean paused briefly in his stride, then said quickly, 'Er, no…no, thank you. I'm afraid that won't be possible at the moment.'

Emma looked at Sean curiously. 'Why not? He's not ill, is he?'

'No…but he wouldn't find it convenient…'

Sean's stilted response seemed out of character, rather terse. Emma wanted to ask exactly why it wasn't convenient for his father to come, but something about Sean's expression deterred her—it was almost as if he didn't want his father to meet her, and for a second she felt quite hurt. Then she chided herself for being stupid and letting her imagination work overtime—what on earth could Mr Casey have against her?

She smiled at him. 'Some other time, then,' she said brightly.

Sean nodded. 'Some other time,' he echoed.

He clenched his fists in his pockets. This was one situation he hadn't thought through—Emma meeting his father. How would his father feel about him going out with Emma Fulford, and how would she feel when she knew about his father's circumstances and just how much their two families had been unwillingly entwined in the past?

CHAPTER EIGHT

EMMA squeezed into the last space in the staff car park and had a quick, guilty look at her watch. Somehow staying in bed with Sean seemed much more attractive these days than getting up early to be in time for work! She paused for a moment and looked across the bay, the sea sparkling in the sun, and already little yachts with coloured sails like butterflies skimming across the water. The scene reflected her mood of happiness and contentment—she could not remember when life had held so much promise for her! She ran lightly up the steps and went through to the casualty department.

Katie looked up as Emma strode past. 'Visitor for you,' she called out. 'He's waiting over there.'

She pointed to a corner of the waiting room and Emma's heart sank when she realised that it was Charles. Why had he come again so early in the day to see her at work? Her serene mood of a few seconds earlier plummeted as she went up to him. He was leaning elegantly back in a chair, reading a newspaper, but stood up languidly when she approached.

'What do you want now?' Emma demanded crossly.

'Don't jump to conclusions, sis. It's only a little thing…'

'It always is, Charles—according to you. And I really don't appreciate you coming to the hospital when I'm working—I'm late as it is. I hope it's not about lending you more money?'

He put up his hands as if to soothe her. 'No, no—just a small amount, Emma. This will clear things once and for all.'

'I've told you, I've given you more than I can afford—there's no more coming out of the pot.'

A genuine look of fear crossed her brother's face and he sat down abruptly.

'Don't abandon me,' he pleaded. 'I know I've got myself into a mess—but I don't want Mother to know. You must help me, please. I've got to get these people off my back, otherwise I could be in real trouble, and I mean *real* trouble! I…I've already been threatened.'

For the first time Emma noticed a bruise on the side of Charles's forehead—an ugly purple bump half-hidden by his hair.

'Did someone beat you up?' she said in a horrified voice.

He shrugged. 'It was a warning—that's the sort of thing they do. They're scum, don't care who they hurt.'

'For God's sake, Charles, why don't you go to the police?'

Again she saw the terror in his eyes. 'That would make it worse, Emma—they'd get me somehow.'

'But surely the money you had from me before will pay your debts?'

'I thought it would do…'

Emma looked at Charles sharply. 'You've gambled it away again, haven't you? You've damn well used my money to fritter it away on a horse.'

'I was onto a cert, Emma—and if it had come home it would have solved everything!'

Emma looked at him in fury. 'How *dare* you?' she

said at last. 'What about little Ben—surely you owe it to him not to get into trouble?'

'I know,' said Charles, hanging his head miserably. 'I swear to God if you help me out this time, I'll never do it again. Please, sis, for old times' sake?'

Emma felt trapped. Just how much danger was Charles in, and how could they keep it from their mother? She sighed and eventually said heavily, 'Just this very last time, then, Charles. This really is it!'

'Thank you, Emma—thank you, darling. I'm so very grateful.' Charles flung his arms round his sister and hugged her to him. 'You won't regret this! And, sis...'

'Yes?'

'You'll keep this to yourself, won't you?'

Emma sighed. 'Of course. Do you think I want anyone to know my brother's managed to gamble away thousands of pounds?'

And the last person she wanted to tell, she thought glumly, was Sean. She knew she was being a fool to subsidize her brother, and Sean might not understand why she was doing it—but she couldn't see her brother in danger, neither could she bear the thought of her mother being involved. The feeling of elation she'd had at the start of the day began to drain away from her, and suddenly the future seemed clouded by worry. Damn her brother and his stupid gambling!

At the door of Reception Sean watched the little tableau in surprise. He'd seen that man in the hospital before speaking to Emma—who the hell was he, and why was he embracing her? He frowned, watching as the man left by the sliding reception doors and Emma walked down the corridor. She looked flustered and upset, and Sean was sure the man had not been a patient—Emma was professional enough to keep her feelings under control at work where patients were concerned. He determined that he would find out just what was going on.

He looked up at the details of patients coming in by ambulance as they flashed up on the screen in the alcove off the main corridor. There were lots of new arrivals, and it looked as if he'd started his shift in the middle of a very busy period—he'd have no time to talk to Emma now. After a short conference with Bob and Connie, he made his way to a cubicle where a man was waiting to be seen with an ankle injury. Tania was dealing with him and her flushed face turned round to greet Sean with relief.

'Ah—Dr Casey. Mr Burton's injured his ankle, running for a train. He says he has no time to have an X-ray, but I've told him that without it it's difficult to distinguish between a bad sprain and a fracture.'

The man looked fretfully at Sean. 'I've been waiting for three hours to get some kind of medical attention. I've got an interview at lunchtime and I'll never make it if I don't get out of here soon. Can't you just put some kind of support on it?'

Sean felt a degree of sympathy for the man—it was hard to be kept waiting that length of time and not feel that one had been completely abandoned.

'I'm sorry, Mr Burton—you've come at a bad time. Lots of emergency cases came in earlier that had to be dealt with first.'

'I've been sitting in that waiting room for ever and I've not seen anyone in dire straits—they've just forgotten about me. Anyway, I'm going to lay a complaint.' The man bit his lip and a look of desperation crossed his face. 'This department's probably ruined the first chance I've had of a job for months—and I really thought my life was turning a corner at last.'

Tania and Sean exchanged glances. Life was unfair sometimes—and although running for a train and tripping wasn't their fault, the fact was that the man might miss out on getting a job because of delays in Casualty.

'I do sympathise, but the ambulances come in the back way, so you wouldn't have seen them arrive,' explained Sean. 'I must recommend, however, that you have an X-ray. I promise it won't take long. While you're waiting we'll put cold compresses on it to try and reduce the swelling. Why don't you ring the people you're going to meet and explain? They may have other interviews that they could bring forward.'

'I'll bring you a phone,' said Tania. 'You can't use a mobile in here.'

Sean looked at the man's contused ankle, hideously swollen and already turning a deep purple.

'You did this running for a train?'

'I was trying to catch it before it left the station and jumped down several steps—my ankle just gave way. If I hadn't been so keen to get there early…' His voice trailed away and he sighed. 'Just my luck.' He glanced at his watch. 'I could do it in quarter of an hour if I got a taxi.'

Tania wheeled in a telephone and Mr Burton stabbed out the numbers—Sean noticed that his hand was trembling. The poor man was in a terrible state.

'Any luck?' he asked Mr Burton as he replaced the handset.

'I've got another half-hour leeway,' the man replied. 'Just bandage me up, will you? And if you've got some crutches I could borrow, I'll come back tomorrow and have the X-ray.'

Sean shrugged. 'If you insist. I can't make you have the X-ray. Sister Cornish will wrap your ankle in a compression bandage, and you ought to keep it raised with ice packs on it tonight—and don't put any weight on it.' He looked kindly at the patient's agitated flushed face. 'Try and keep calm—and good luck at your interview.'

'I'll need it,' said Mr Burton with a hollow laugh. 'If I don't get this job my wife says she'll leave me. We've got three kids and a mortgage to pay.'

He slumped back on the bed and closed his eyes as Tania started to bandage his ankle, and Sean went to the vending machine in the corridor, returning a few minutes later with a steaming cup of tea.

'Take a few sips of this, Mr Burton. It's rather like instant sludge, but it might help relax you.'

Mr Burton looked at him in grateful surprise. 'Why, thank you very much. I could do with that. I...I'm sorry I was a bit off before—it's just absolutely typical that I should mess up with an interview.'

'Cheer up, man,' said Sean with a grin. 'You haven't failed it yet—and perhaps they'll be impressed that you made it after all, even with a crocked ankle!'

'Wait here while I find you some crutches,' said Tania.

She and Sean went out of the cubicle together and Sean said wryly, 'You certainly get to know about people's troubles in this job!'

Connie appeared, coming up to him at a pace. 'Sean, can you come quickly and help Emma? I've a woman in Resus who could be in anaphylactic shock. Zak's brought her in on a trolley from the car park, and her partner's with her in a distressed state. Most of us are dealing with two RTA victims in the small theatre and there's a suspected cardiac arrest coming in any minute.'

Sean sprinted through to the resuscitation room, taking in at a glance a woman lying on the trolley with a swollen face and blue lips, her limbs twitching spasmodically. She was breathing stertorously, choking and wheezing—every breath a supreme effort. Emma was trying to put a plastic airway into the woman's throat and a terrified-looking man was standing at the side of the room, watching her as if mesmerised.

'This is difficult to insert,' Emma said grimly. 'Her tongue and throat are very swollen... Ah... Thank goodness—that's done it.' She turned to Bill. 'Raise her legs and let's give her some extra fluid....she's in shock.'

'What's she taken?' Sean asked the man who'd brought her in. He pulled back the lid of the patient's eyes and looked at the pupils, nodding up at Emma as if in confirmation. 'Her pupils are dilated—she's had a massive reaction to something.'

'Oh, God, will she be all right?' whispered the man, twisting his hands frantically together.

'Do you know what she's had?' repeated Sean loudly, trying to drag the man's attention back from the distressed patient.

'She took one of my tablets. I told her not to—but she said it would help her cystitis.'

'Well, go on, man—what kind of a tablet?'

'It was something the doctor gave me for a sore

throat…penicillin it was. I told her not to have it,' he repeated hopelessly.

'Hell,' swore Sean under his breath. 'Get some epinephrine into her pronto, Emma—we've got to keep her airways open. Set up a saline drip to try and reverse the shock. We'd better have some oxygen as well. What's her heart rate?'

'One forty-five and rising…'

'Give her some Benadryl after the epinephrine.'

Sean started to press on the woman's chest, trying to help her breathing, while Emma gave the first injection and then prepared the second. After both injections had been given she put a clamp on the feed line from the saline bag and injected the needle into a vein in the patient's arm.

'This had better work,' she murmured.

She stood back, willing the drugs to reverse the reaction the woman had suffered, watching her like a hawk.

'What's happening?' squeaked the man behind them. 'Is she getting better?'

Sean didn't reply for a few seconds, then he took a deep breath. 'I think she is,' he said softly, listening to her heart through his stethoscope. 'Respiration, pulse going down. She's breathing more easily… I think we're in luck this time.'

Gradually the laboured breathing became easier and the twitching of the woman's limbs subsided. Emma blew out her cheeks in relief and turned to the man watching them nervously.

'I hope you've both learnt something,' she said drily. 'Remember, the pills were only prescribed for you—

you can see how dangerous it can be for someone else to take them.'

'I know,' said the man miserably. 'I tried to stop her, but she said she was desperate, and they didn't seem to do me any harm.'

'I'm afraid a few people react badly—their immune system attacks the penicillin and their heart gets starved of oxygen. Next time she has an infection tell her to go to the doctor for a prescription.'

'We're going on holiday to Spain later today. She hadn't time to go to the doctor.'

'I don't think she'll be going anywhere today except an observation ward,' said Sean. 'Your girlfriend needs watching for forty-eight hours just to make sure she's OK—she's not up to travelling yet. She's had a very violent allergic reaction.'

'I did try and stop her,' repeated the man. 'Ah, well, it's a good job it didn't happen in the hotel after we'd arrived.'

'Or, worse, on the plane,' interjected Emma. 'There might not have been such a happy outcome.'

Zak came in to take the girl to the ward and when he'd gone Sean shook his head at Emma.

'That was a close call,' he remarked. 'How stupid can people get? There's enough warnings on the bottles about not taking medication unless it's been prescribed for you. If she'd been brought in ten minutes later she might not have survived.'

'I know. It doesn't bear thinking about.' Emma flicked a look at her watch. 'I must make a phone call after all the majors have been cleared,' she said.

'How about coffee in half an hour or so when the panic's died down a bit? I want to talk to you anyway.'

Emma shook her head and sounded distracted. 'I'll see... If I've time, perhaps.'

'Something urgent?' Sean enquired lightly.

Emma bit her lip and frowned. 'Not really—just something I've got to sort out...'

He smiled. 'You seem rather mysterious, sweetheart. Are you worried about anything?'

'No...not at all. I'll see you soon...but don't wait for me.'

She walked briskly out of the room, preventing further discussion, but instinctively Sean knew that the phone call was related to the man he'd seen her with. Ah, well, he thought wryly, he'd catch up with her later and find out more.

Emma wrinkled her nose. The canteen had the familiar smell of stale cabbage and rather greasy chips which, unless one was very hungry, was enough to put one off food completely. Charles's visit had unsettled her, and she certainly didn't feel like eating anything, but after the busy morning she'd had and the equally busy afternoon in front of her, she reckoned she'd better have something to keep her going.

Sean waved at Emma from the other side of the room and she went over to him—rather reluctantly. The phone call to her bank manager authorising the movement of all her savings to her current account had been depressing, and she felt she needed her own space for a while. She knew that she was being foolish to lend her brother more money—yet how much trouble would he be in if she didn't help him?

With a sigh, Emma sat down in the chair Sean pulled out for her. He glanced at her assessingly, taking in her preoccupied expression, her pale face and set lips. She seemed very different from the high-spirited girl he'd had breakfast with.

'Let me get you something, sweetheart. A bacon buttie? An omelette?'

Emma shook her head. 'No, thanks...I'm really not very hungry. A cup of tea and piece of toast would be fine.'

He frowned. 'You'll get hypoglycaemic, Dr Fulford. Why have you lost your appetite? It's not like you.'

'It...it's nothing. I only feel like a snack.'

Sean looked at her with a raised brow. 'Come on, Emma, something's bothering you, isn't it?'

Emma was silent. 'Only a minor worry,' she said at last. 'I'm sure it'll be resolved.'

Sean leaned forward in his chair and touched her cheek. 'I thought we were to have no secrets,' he said gently. 'Anyway, a trouble shared is a trouble halved.'

His eyes were full of kindness, and to her horror Emma felt a well of tears spring up in her eyes. How ridiculous it was—to get in such a state about her brother. It must be because she'd had a gruelling morning at work and was tired, or perhaps it was Sean's concern. She took out her handkerchief and blew her nose.

'I told you—it's nothing, Sean. I'm just being silly.'

'I saw you earlier with that man who's accosted you before in the hospital—it's to do with him, isn't it?'

Emma stared at him in shocked surprise. 'Why...why do you think that?'

'I saw your face when you walked away from him—you looked upset. What the hell's going on, Emma? Is he blackmailing you or something?'

For a random shot it was pretty near the mark. Emma flushed and said miserably, 'The man is my brother. He's in a spot of bother—I suppose I'm worried about him.'

'Ah…what kind of bother?'

'I don't want to talk about it, Sean. Suffice it to say that he's been a fool.'

Sean drummed his fingers on the table. 'Emma, I care too much for you to let it go at that. For heaven's sake, tell me.' He looked at her with a grin. 'It can't be that bad—he hasn't murdered anyone, has he?'

Emma gave a faint smile. 'Not quite as bad as that…no.'

'Then tell me. I shan't let it rest until you do. I can't bear you to look so worried.'

Sean's deep blue eyes held hers for a minute and she sighed helplessly. She did need to talk things over with someone—and why not Sean?

'The fact is,' she said slowly, 'he's got himself into debt. He's been gambling and of course he owes money and he's been chased for that. He doesn't want my mother to know either…'

'So he came to you and you've been giving him money, have you?' asked Sean in a grim voice.

She looked at him pleadingly. 'I've got to help him, Sean. He's in big trouble, and he is my brother.'

Sean shook his head. 'The fact is, you're feeding his gambling habit—and how stupid is that? It could go on for ever! You have to be firm.'

Emma flushed. 'I thought you might understand why I was helping him, Sean. I felt I had no other choice.'

'Of course you had a choice.' Sean's voice was hard. 'You'll get dragged into trouble with him if you're not careful, and he'll always be asking you for money. Don't give him any more, Emma—he'll be coming to you for the rest of his life.'

'I know you're right. I'm just worried about what will happen to him. I know he's being threatened by moneylenders,' she said miserably.

'Then, for goodness' sake, do the right thing—forget about him!'

A sudden feeling of resentment flared in Emma. Sean might be right, but Charles was her brother after all and for all his faults she couldn't see him in danger. A stubborn look crossed her face.

'I don't need to be told what to do—you're not my keeper, Sean. You mustn't bully me to do what you want.'

'Don't be ridiculous, Emma. I want what's best for you.'

'You sound just like my father—and I'm not a child any more.'

Sean's mouth tightened and his voice held a hint of anger, although he spoke softly. 'Don't compare me to your father, sweetheart—I don't *ever* want to be identified with a man like him!'

Emma's eyes sparked angrily across at him, offended by Sean's tone. 'What on earth do you mean? Just why do you hate him as much as you do? You've made it clear before that you and he didn't get on. He could be arrogant, yes, and he bullied me—but he was a damn good doctor, someone who dragged themselves up from a very poor background, and I admired him for it!'

Sean looked at her silently, appalled that the atmosphere between them had suddenly plunged to several degrees below freezing.

He put his hand over hers on the table and said softly, 'What the hell are we quarrelling about, Emma? This is so ridiculous.'

She had never looked lovelier, he thought. Anger had darkened her brown eyes and her cheeks were flushed, her hair tousled. He longed to take her in his arms.

She snatched her hand away from his. 'I'm not quarrelling—I just need to know why my father is such a hate figure in your eyes.'

Telling Emma about just why he hated Professor Fulford might not be a good idea he reflected wryly, and yet if he kept quiet might it all not come out at a later date?

Emma leaned forward and smacked her hand on the table impatiently. 'Come on, Sean, I thought we were going to be open with each other—no secrets and all that?'

'I can't tell you here—not near all these people,' he said rather desperately, looking round the canteen.

'For heaven's sake, the place is nearly empty,' said Emma through gritted teeth. 'Tell me now before I go mad!'

'Very well, then,' Sean said, grim-faced. 'You won't like what you're going to hear, though...' He took a deep breath and began slowly, 'There's no easy way to tell this, but I'm afraid to say that some years ago your father was the cause of untold unhappiness. He ruined our family.'

Emma looked at him, astonished. 'What do you mean?'

'To put it baldly, he had an affair with my mother...my father and he had been friends at university together and they met up again about three years ago. He led my mother to believe that he would leave his wife—but he never had any intention of doing so.'

The breath seemed to leave Emma's body and her heart thudded with shock. Her father having an affair? The man who had been so strict with them as children, so scornful of people who 'messed up their lives', as he'd put it.

'I...I don't believe it,' whispered Emma, white-faced. 'He couldn't have done!'

Sean shook his head. 'I wish it wasn't true—but the fact is, my mother left my father because of Professor Fulford. My father was broken-hearted and it ruined him. He turned to drink and he hates meeting anyone now. Of course, my mother was at fault as well—but your father had a dominant personality and could persuade people to do what he wanted them to do.'

He paused for a moment and looked sadly at Emma. 'Can you understand what it was like, working with your father and knowing all this? It didn't make for an easy relationship, I can tell you.'

A cold feeling of horror crept through Emma's body and she looked at Sean wordlessly. Her mind seemed to be in freefall, unable to think properly. Suddenly her world had changed in a few seconds—her father had broken up a family, her brother was set to ruin his own life. She put her hands over her face and started to weep.

'How could he?' she whispered. 'How could he betray my mother and yours?'

Sean got up and came to sit by her, putting his arm

round her. 'Sweetheart...please, don't cry. I don't blame you—it's not your fault.'

She pulled away from him, looking at him with red-rimmed eyes. 'Don't be so damned patronising. I know it's not my fault, but it doesn't make me feel any better, knowing my own father hurt so many people.'

He spread his hands helplessly. 'Whatever I say will be wrong, Emma. I'm sorry.'

Emma sighed. 'I know, I know. Now I can see why you didn't want your father to meet me—he would hate me on sight if he knew who I was!'

'It might be difficult at first,' admitted Sean, 'but I know he'd grow to love you like I do—given time. But I can never forgive your father. Breaking up families is totally immoral in my book—destroying their lives is a wicked thing to do.'

Emma heart began to beat so hard that she could hardly breathe. She stared at him strangely, then stood up. 'You're right, Sean,' she said in a small voice. 'It was a wicked thing. I...I'm sorry, but this is all rather much for me at the moment.'

'Where are you going?'

'I'm going back to work. And, Sean...don't expect me to stay with you tonight—or in the future.' A sob caught in her voice.

Sean sprang up and held her shoulders, forcing her to look at him. 'What are you talking about? For heaven's sake, this mustn't break us up. It was in the past, nothing to do with you!'

Gently she disengaged her shoulders from his grasp. 'Maybe not. Nevertheless, I can't live with you, Sean.' She looked at him with anguished eyes. 'It...it wouldn't work any more. You hate what my father did—understandably...'

'Yes, it was very wrong. But that's not your fault. I love you, believe me.' He tilted her face towards his and said softly. 'Surely the past few days have demonstrated that, sweetheart?'

His lips were so close to hers, lips that had kissed her so passionately only the night before. If she closed her eyes she could almost feel his rough chin against her cheek, smell the male smell of him, imagine his hard body pressed to hers. How wonderful life and the future had seemed just a few short hours ago! Then she pushed those thoughts resolutely to the back of her mind. Things had changed now—they could never be as they once were.

'How can I believe you?' she said sadly. 'I'll not be able to stop thinking about your father whenever I look at you. And besides...' Her voice faltered and stopped.

'Besides what? You can't let this come between us, my darling...please. I know it's a shock for you, but you'll get over it...' He looked at her sadly. 'I should never have told you...'

Emma shook her head. 'I had to know eventually, and you don't understand, Sean. You see, if you knew what I was really like you might hate me as much as you do my father!'

She turned and almost ran out of the cafeteria, pushing aside tables and chairs in her haste to get away from Sean and his stricken face.

Dammit, he thought miserably, sinking down into his chair again and gazing unseeingly ahead of him. He should have waited to tell Emma about her father—not chosen a time when she was especially vulnerable over her brother's stupidity. And as for hating her—whatever she'd done, he loved her more than ever. How stupid he'd been to talk about the past—and how on earth could he mend fences between them again, just when everything had seemed so perfect?

CHAPTER NINE

IT HAD been a long miserable week. Emma had avoided Sean as much as possible at work, and when they had met it had been as if she'd worked with a stranger. She felt a mixture of shame and incomprehension at her father's actions. Professor Fulford had been held in such esteem by the hospital, despite his shortcomings. How could he have risked his reputation by having a sordid affair, and how could he have betrayed her mother who had supported him during the lean years of his career?

Emma wondered if her mother knew about it and suspected that she did, recalling the bitter tone in her voice when she had first told her of her meeting with Sean Casey. Her mother had mentioned some quarrel between her father and Sean—but maybe that had just been a front to hide the real story.

Despite the work that had needed to be done on it after the storm, Emma had moved back into her cottage. She had left a note for Sean, saying that she thought it better that they let things cool off between them for a bit, and had added lightly that she would 'see him at work, no doubt.' Every night he had rung her, but she'd left the phone on the answering-machine and had never rung him back. Neither had she answered any of the notes he'd put through the door. She felt totally empty and battered, convinced that if Sean despised her father for his actions, he would equally despise her if he knew the background of her affair with Mike.

She gazed morosely out of the kitchen window in Casualty, holding a cup of cold coffee in her hand, and swore softly to herself.

Just when I thought I had my life back on track and had found my ideal man, she reflected sadly.

The door slammed behind her and Tania came in, flopping down on a chair and fanning her face with a tissue.

'Why is it always hot when we're working?' she complained. 'When I've a free day it teems with rain and the kids are stuck inside, driving me mad. '

Emma nodded absently, and Tania looked at her thoughtfully. 'You don't seem your usual cheery self, love,' she commented. 'Is it work, or has someone been upsetting you?'

'No—not work,' said Emma lightly.

'Then it's someone like Dr Sean Casey perhaps?' she said shrewdly.

Emma's head snapped round and stared at Tania suspiciously. 'What...what do you mean, Tania, "like Dr Sean Casey"?'

Tania laughed. 'Anyone would have to be a blind fool not to notice that you and he have the hots for one another. He never takes his eyes off you, and when you come into the room he lights up like a beacon. So what's happened? All not sweetness and light in the land of Cupid?'

'I didn't realise you knew,' muttered Emma. 'And to tell you the truth, everything's pretty awful between us at the moment—in fact, I can't see that we'll ever get back together again!'

Tania handed Emma a fresh cup of coffee and looked at her sympathetically. 'What's gone wrong, love? Tell Auntie Tania all about it…I'm good at giving advice!'

Emma shook her head. 'I can't tell you, Tania. It's to do with something that happened a long time ago, something horrible… And we had such a lot going for us,' she added wistfully.

'If it happened ages ago then I should put it behind you and get on with your life,' said Tania firmly. 'For heaven's sake, don't let someone gorgeous like Sean Casey slip through your fingers. In any case, I think you're made for each other!'

Emma gave a faint smile. 'I thought we were too… Perhaps I was wrong.'

'You go and make up with him, Emma. Don't let old history spoil the present. Anyway, it's awful having the two of you moping around like lost souls. Now,' she added briskly, 'I expect to hear a good report from you tomorrow—so think about it!'

She paused before she swept out of the room and said as an afterthought, 'Don't forget it's Bill Taylor's leaving party in a few days' time—there's going to be a disco. You'll be coming, won't you?'

Emma sighed. 'I suppose so—although the last thing I feel like after a day here is being energetic.'

'You're beginning to sound like an old woman,' said Tania. 'You'll be OK after a glass of the best wine Carrfield General has to offer!'

She went out and despite herself Emma gave a chuckle. Tania was a refreshing character and said what she thought, but Emma still felt the shock of Sean's revelations. Whatever Tania said about them being made for each other, Emma reflected, she had to cut Sean out of her life now. Too much baggage from the past had been disturbed. Her family was bad news, she thought with shame—all of them, her father, her brother and herself!

The sudden squeal of the cardiac alarm jerked her back to the present, and with the automatic response of long training Emma raced towards the resus room in the majors area. She almost bumped into Sean coming from the other direction with Bill. Their eyes met for a startled second before they entered the room, then they became part of the co-ordinated group that made up the crash team. Briefly Emma felt a lump come into her throat at the sight of Sean in his hospital greens, his athletic broad figure dwarfing everyone else around him, and as they crowded round the patient's bed she wondered bleakly how could she endure a future without him. Then guiltily she pushed the thought away and concentrated on helping Albert Shields to keep a hold on life as he battled with a major heart attack.

Bert was a big man, about twenty stone, and he was in great pain, his eyes closed, his hands clenched, the centre of a drama which an hour ago he wouldn't have dreamed of when he'd been wandering happily round a garden centre with his wife.

Connie was listening to his chest, her eyes flicking up as the team entered the room. Albert was already hooked up to a monitor, the electrocardiograph trace showing the thready irregular line of his labouring heart.

'Ventricular fibrillation big time,' she murmured. 'Can you get a bigger airway in, Emma? And let's get some bloods done and drugs into him.'

For a few seconds the room seemed chaotic as the team sprang to carry out procedures, but underneath the frantic activity there was a co-ordinated plan of action as everyone carried out his or her task.

'Right,' said Sean briskly. 'We'll have four mils lignocaine, please, Bill.'

He pulled back Albert's eyelids and examined his pupils as Bill undid the roll of prepacked injectible drugs from the cardiac box and selected the right syringe.

'Where was Mr Shields when this happened?' he asked, taking the syringe from Bill and injecting it into Albert's upper arm.

'In a garden centre with his wife. Apparently he'd just been loading heavy bags of compost into his car and he collapsed with chest pains.'

Sean grunted. 'Poor fellow—gardening can be a dangerous pastime.' He looked down at the prone figure before him, anonymous under the oxygen mask, and said clearly, 'Hang on there, Albert. We're helping you here—you should feel less pain soon…'

Albert stirred slightly and groaned.

'Hopefully this lignocaine will get his cardiac rhythm back. Has he had aspirin or streptokinase?'

'Yes,' replied Bill. 'Ten thousand units streptokinase and 300 mils aspirin on admittance, and ten thousand units heparin in the ambulance.'

'No response—it's still all over the place,' said Connie tersely as she listened to the heart through her stethoscope. 'We're going to have to shock him. Emma, can you take the paddles?'

Emma unhooked the paddles from the defibrillation

machine and placed them under the heart and on the upper right of the chest.

'Everyone stand back,' she said loudly. 'Charging now—200 joules.'

There was silence except for the movement of the bulky body of Albert Shields as he shuddered and arched when the current was activated, then Connie listened again to his chest.

'Try again. I think it's doing its job...'

Emma repeated the procedure and again the silence was palpable as the team willed Albert's heart to jerk into rhythm again. Then Connie straightened up and puffed out her cheeks in relief.

'It's worked! Give him some oxygen and get him down to CCU a.s.a.p. Check his blood gases for acidity.'

'His wife's in the relatives' waiting room,' said Bill as he pushed the defibrillator back against the wall. 'Could someone go and talk to her?'

'I'll go,' said Emma. She needed to get out of the same room as Sean now they'd finished with their patient, and do something quickly to take her mind off him.

Mrs Shields was as tiny as her husband was large. She perched on the edge of a chair in the waiting room reserved for relatives of gravely ill patients, looking like a small bewildered bird. In a few short minutes, having a pleasant morning out, her world had turned upside down. As Emma entered the room she looked up anxiously.

'Is he all right? What's happening?' she said in a voice that cracked with tension.

Emma smiled at her and sat down beside the frightened woman. She could imagine how worried Mrs Shields had been and the shock she'd had to endure, seeing her husband collapse.

'I'm Dr Fulford and I've been in the resus room with your husband,' she explained. 'The news so far is good in that he seems reasonably stable at the moment. He's been taken to the coronary care unit.'

'But he'll recover, won't he?' Mrs Shields's anxious eyes raked Emma's face, her hands twisting together nervously.

'Mr Shields is still seriously ill,' Emma said cautiously, not giving false hope to the woman. 'He's had a major heart attack, but he'll be watched like a hawk from now on, although it may be a long haul—for both of you!'

'I told him to take off weight,' said Mrs Shields tearfully. 'But he likes his food does Albert—and his beer...'

'Well, perhaps now he'll take some notice of your advice,' said Emma gently. 'Anyway, I'm sure the cardiac consultant will be talking to him and suggesting things he can do in the future to help himself.'

Mrs Shields dabbed at her eyes with a handkerchief. 'I...I'm sorry, Doctor, I feel a fool, crying. It's just that it's been such a shock. One minute we were as happy as sandboys, buying plants at the garden centre—he loves his garden—and the next thing he'd collapsed by the car. I didn't know what to do.'

Emma nodded, letting Mrs Shields describe the events leading up to her husband's attack. It would do her good to express her feelings and help her to cope later.

'At least he was brought to hospital very quickly,'

she said comfortingly. 'The sooner these patients are seen, the better. Have you anyone you should contact about this—children or a friend that might sit with you for a while? Would you like me to ring them for you? In the meantime, you can go to Coronary Care and you may be able to see your husband.'

Bill popped his head round the door. 'Would Mrs Shields like a cup of tea perhaps?' he asked.

'Thank you, I'd love a cup,' whispered the little lady. 'You...you've all been so kind. I'll ring my sister myself and wait here till she comes.'

Emma smiled as she left the room. The wonderful power of a cup of tea to comfort and sustain was remarkable! Then the smile faded from her face and she swallowed nervously when she saw that Sean was outside the door, leaning against the wall. He stepped forward and held her arm firmly, starting to lead her down the corridor.

'We need to talk, you and I,' he said. He opened the door of a room used for staff meetings and conferences. 'There's no one in here—everyone's having coffee at the moment.'

'Not just now,' pleaded Emma, hanging back. 'Anyway, there's nothing to talk about. What's happened can't be undone.'

He closed the door behind him and leant against it, folding his arms and looking at her with his clear blue eyes.

'Be real, Emma. Think how close we've been for the last few weeks. We just can't turn things off as if we were robots. What's going on? Why haven't you returned my calls or answered my notes?'

Emma felt the heat rising in her face. She felt

trapped, too close to Sean and afraid she would have to confess the real cause for leaving him.

'You know why I haven't been in touch,' she said a shade desperately. 'How can we possibly stay together after what my father did to your family?'

'I told you—that makes no difference to me.' He stepped nearer to her and gazed at her intently. 'I love you like crazy, and I'm not letting this come between us.'

Emma's stomach felt as though a hundred butterflies were fluttering inside. His words spun round in her mind. He loved her and she loved him with all her heart—but he didn't know the true Emma.

He put his hands on her shoulders and she closed her eyes. It was almost unbearable to have him so close to her without flinging her arms around him and pulling that hard body close to hers.

'Don't touch me, Sean. I can't bear it if you do...' Her voice wobbled and she bit her lip. 'You hate what my father did and so do I. It will always come between our two families.'

'I don't care a hang what our families think,' he said roughly. 'Why can't you see that it's over and done with as far as we're concerned? Your father and my mother are dead—we've got to forget what happened between them. I only told you because you asked why I hated him so much.'

'It's not that easy,' she murmured, and looked up at him sadly. 'I want us to part on good terms—please, don't prolong things.'

He shook his head in exasperation and his voice was rough. 'I don't understand you, Emma. Is there something I don't know?'

Was this the moment, Emma thought, the time to tell him precisely why he would want to leave her if he knew? Some remnant of self-respect kept her silent—she still needed him to think well of her.

With an exclamation of impatience he put his arms round her and then his lips were on hers, bruising and passionate. She couldn't help the thrill that tingled through every nerve end and opened her lips to his demanding mouth, arching her body in response to his hands as they wandered possessively over her curves.

'Come back to me, Emma, love,' he whispered. 'Forget what I told you. Let's be together again, doing this whenever we want to...'

Emma melted against him, her willpower fading very quickly, and for a wild moment the fleeting thought crossed her mind that they might lie down there and then on the floor and make love in the conference room—and she would do nothing to stop him! A surge of hysterical laughter began to bubble up inside her. This was too ridiculous, but it was unimaginably wonderful to be back in Sean's arms again. Why should she spoil things between them? Perhaps she need never tell him about her past with Mike after all?

The sudden insistent sound of Emma's bleeper was like an alarm call that brought her back to harsh reality. She pulled away from Sean with a dazed expression, as if she'd woken from a dream.

'Oh, lord, what the hell are we doing—here in the hospital? We must be mad! I...I must go and find out what that is,' she said, a sense of relief flooding through her at the interruption.

Sean sighed and let her go reluctantly. 'You've got

to come back to me,' he said quietly. 'I know you want to...'

Emma pushed passed him and opened the door. 'It's time for work, Sean,' she said hastily. 'We'll talk again some other time.'

She smoothed down her hospital greens and dashed down the corridor.

Bill was talking to a woman outside one of the treatment bays, and turned to Emma as she hurried towards them.

'Ah, Dr Fulford, you heard me bleeping you. This is Mrs Lawton. She's just brought in her little boy, Jonty. He's six years old and he's been bitten by a snake—an adder bite. His arm's swelling rapidly and we've put him in number one bay.'

'Are you certain it was an adder?' asked Emma.

'Quite sure,' said Mrs Lawton, turning to look at Emma. 'My neighbour verified it from a book he has by the description Jonty gave.'

She was tall, young and blonde and very attractive. Emma stared at her for a second in stupefied disbelief and a little shock wave of recognition ran through her body. A few years ago she had occasionally seen Mrs Lawton from a distance at a party or sometimes shopping at the local supermarket. Now she was face to face with her, hardly able to take in what the woman was saying, hardly able to believe that this was the wife of her old lover Mike, standing before her.

This was a scenario she could never have envisaged, she thought bitterly. She had believed that Mike had moved away after she and he had split up. She had certainly never dreamed that she would one day be treating his son!

She swallowed hard, forcing herself to remain professional, objective.

'Right, Mrs Lawton,' she said briskly, hiding her inner turmoil as well as she could. 'Let's go and see Jonty, and tell me exactly what happened.'

A little boy with a shock of red hair and a freckled face was whimpering on the bed, his swollen red arm resting on the sheet. Emma noted he was pale and sweaty, eyelids drooping.

'I feel sick,' he whispered. 'I want some water.'

'We'll give you some water, Jonty,' said Emma reassuringly, putting a hand on his damp forehead. 'What's his BP and heart rate, Bill?'

'BP's falling, pulse increasing—130 at the moment.'

'Right. He needs some tetanus antitoxin and antibiotics immediately to knock out the possibility of infection, and ring the path lab for antivenin. Get it sent over immediately. In the meantime, I'll do his bloods to check for D dimers.'

'Wh-what's that for?' stammered Mrs Lawton.

'It's to measure the clotting factor in his blood—we call it disseminated intravascular coagulation, or DIC. The bruising you see round Jonty's arm probably means he's bleeding into the tissue. How long ago was he bitten?'

'About twenty minutes ago. We'd come over to see his grandmother for a few days, and he was playing in the long grass at the bottom of her garden. I just bundled him in the car and came here as soon as I could.'

There was a tremor in the woman's voice, but she tried to maintain her composure. 'I didn't know if I was overreacting,' she added, 'but his arm seemed to swell so quickly.'

'You did the right thing Mrs Lawton,' said Emma.

'Please, call me Leanne.'

But of course, thought Emma wryly, I know your name so well. Leanne Lawton—the woman she used to envy because she had everything that she herself wanted in life. Emma looked at Leanne now. She had the terrified, bewildered look of most mothers when their children were brought in with acute illness. As a parent they were out of control, and unable to help the most precious thing in their lives.

'Sit down, Leanne,' she said gently. 'Hold Jonty's other hand and talk to him. He needs to know you're there for him, even if the poison makes him drowsy.'

Emma took a felt-tip pen out of her pocket and marked a line on the child's arm where the angry red mark on his skin stopped.

'We can tell how quickly the swelling is progressing if we mark it,' she explained. 'We're also monitoring his blood with a pulse oximeter—the machine by his bed—for oxygen levels.'

Sean came in, his solid presence comforting in the small room. 'Do you need anything?' he asked Emma.

She nodded and said in a low voice as she noted the readings of his oxygen levels, 'Ring HDU, will you? I think he needs close monitoring. If his toxicity levels increase too much I don't want to take the chance that his respiratory system gets distressed without back-up.'

Then she turned back to Leanne Lawton. 'Just to be on the safe side, we're going to send Jonty to the high-dependency unit for a while.'

Leanne made a little sound of distress. 'Is it very serious, then?' she said shakily.

'Bringing him in so quickly was the best thing you

could have done. However, he is only a little boy and the venomous dose he's had works quicker on a small body mass. We need to be ready to give him emergency treatment if he should need it.'

Emma bent forward over Jonty's arm and looked closely at his hand. She pointed to his finger.

'See those two little marks there? Those are the puncture wounds of the adder's fangs. It's lucky that he's been bitten on his right hand—the left-hand side has direct blood circulation to the heart and that would have spread the poison much more quickly.'

'Oh, God, it's my fault.' Leanne buried her head in her hands and her voice was muffled. 'I should never have told him to go outside. He wanted to stay in and watch some silly programme on TV, but I made him go out because it was such a nice day. He...he picked the snake up—he thought it was a huge worm.'

Emma shook her head. 'Of course it's not your fault—it's just a horrible coincidence that Jonty happened to be in the same place as the snake. It was probably basking in the sun.'

She looked closely at Jonty's arm again. The swelling had moved up the arm even in the few minutes they'd been talking, and the skin looked bruised as the venom prevented the blood from clotting.

Sean came in with Zak. 'They're ready for Jonty in HDU,' he said. 'His mum can go too and sit with him.'

Leanne stood up and dabbed at her eyes with her handkerchief. 'Thank you so much,' she said tearfully. 'I'm really grateful to you.'

'They'll watch Jonty like a hawk,' said Emma comfortingly. 'He couldn't be in a better place.'

'I know—and I feel all the better for that.' Leanne

paused and looked at Emma with a slight frown. 'It's funny, I feel I know your face from somewhere—have we met before?'

Emma's face flamed. 'I…I'm not sure. You don't live round here, do you?'

'No—not now. We moved from here a few years ago. I loved it by the sea, but my husband moved jobs. Perhaps you knew him? He was a medical rep and used to visit this hospital at one time.'

'I think I may have done.' Emma's voice was light despite her dry mouth. 'Is he still a medical rep, then?'

Leanne sighed. 'I've no idea, and I don't care. After we moved he very soon became my ex-husband.' She glanced at her little boy now being transferred to a trolley and lowered her voice slightly. 'He was a womaniser,' she said simply. 'I knew he'd had someone when he worked here. That's why I divorced him.'

The words 'ex-husband' echoed horribly in Emma's ears, and she swallowed hard, trying to come to terms with the revelation that the man who'd kept her dangling on a string for so long had in the end been dumped by his wife. And, she thought with anguish, it was her, Emma's, fault! It was like a knife twisting in her heart to think she'd been the cause of so much unhappiness. How easily she'd been taken in, how stupid!

'I…I'm so sorry you're alone,' she said inadequately.

'It doesn't bother me now. We weren't right for each other anyway, I always knew that,' said Leanne with a philosophical shrug. 'I'm better off without him. I don't think he was ever the marrying kind anyway!' She looked lovingly at Jonty. 'My only concern now is Jonty and his health.'

'Of course it is. And try not to worry, Leanne—they will do their very best for him.'

Zak started to push the little boy to the special unit and Leanne held his good hand as they walked away, talking softly to him.

Emma stared after her, raw emotions tearing her mind apart. Now, having met Mike's ex-wife and son, she realised with a horrible clarity just how blinkered she'd been when she'd been involved with Mike. He had been a rat, incapable of loyalty or love to anyone. He hadn't deserved his lovely wife and child.

'So you met Mrs Lawton's husband, then? He sounds pretty much a scumbag!' Sean's deep voice was behind her, intruding into her thoughts. 'What did you think of him?'

'I didn't know he was like that.' Emma's voice was strained. 'He worked for a company that sold specialist scalpels.'

And I should have used one to cut him out of my life, she thought savagely. Her hands shook as she started to write up Jonty's notes.

Sean looked at her sharply, noting the tone of her voice.

'You OK, Emma?' He tilted her head up to his gaze, then he looked at her, concerned. 'What is it, love? You've been crying, haven't you? What's happened?'

Emma sat down weakly on the chair by the bed. 'It's just been brought home to me,' she whispered, 'how very very foolish I was to think that Mike would ever marry me.'

Sean frowned. 'Your old boyfriend? What's brought this on? I thought you'd got over him.'

'Oh, I did—long ago!' said Emma tremulously. 'But suddenly everything's come flooding back and made me realise just how thoughtless I was. You see, Mike and I both betrayed Leanne and little Jonty!'

'The woman I've just seen?' said Sean in a mystified tone.

'Leanne Lawton was Mike's wife! That's right, Sean—I went out with a married man. I'm just as bad as my father was—like father, like daughter, I'm afraid!'

CHAPTER TEN

SEAN looked at Emma blankly for a second, then he said slowly, 'So this was your little secret—the story you were keeping from me?'

She reddened. 'We said we'd be open with each other, didn't we? I guess until I saw Leanne Lawton I had hoped that episode in my life was over and done with.' She clenched her hands by her side. 'Now I've seen her, the whole thing has come flooding back. But I didn't do it deliberately, you know. I didn't realise Mike was married at first.'

'Sounds a familiar story,' Sean commented drily. 'And when you found out he was married, did you tell him he was a naughty boy and continue to see him—have an affair with him—even though you knew he had a wife?'

'He told me the marriage was over, that he was deeply unhappy. He said…he said he was waiting for a divorce.'

'And you fell for that old line, did you? I'd have thought you would have been more astute than that, Emma!'

'When you think you're in love, astuteness doesn't come into it,' Emma said sadly. 'I really believed he and his wife were living apart. Then…'

'Then what?' prompted Sean.

'I saw them together in a supermarket—it was then that I realised they had a child. Later I was at the same hospital do as they were—he didn't know I'd seen them. When I questioned him later, he said his wife hadn't been well so he'd gone back to live with her temporarily.'

'You were rather gullible, weren't you? How long did your affair continue?'

'About a year,' said Emma miserably. 'He seemed so plausible, I believed every word! He told me he wanted to leave his wife but it was never the right time to do so. He made it seem as if he was the victim—trapped by circumstances in an unhappy marriage.'

'But he got his divorce in the end...'

Something inside Emma snapped and she leapt up from her seat and looked at him with anguished eyes. 'For God's sake, Sean, don't you realise that I've never stopped feeling guilty? Going out with a married man was the stupidest thing I've ever done—someone was bound to get hurt. You know that only too well.' She looked down at her hands and bit her lip. 'I suppose I believed him because I wanted what he said to be true—that his marriage was dead. I didn't set out deliberately to hurt anyone.'

'So now your guilt has flooded back?'

'Sean, I've just met his wife and his little boy—I'd never met them face to face before or heard her side of the story. And now I know what my father did to your family, well...' She looked at the expression on Sean's face and said bitterly, 'That's why I can't stay with you...'

'I don't blame you, Emma. It isn't you I blame at all...'

Tears started coursing down her cheeks and she

brushed them aside impatiently. 'You're saying that—but you're not *thinking* that, are you?'

She walked to the door, then turned to face him with a twisted little smile on her face. 'I'm getting out of your life, Sean. You don't have to pretend to love me any more. I'm leaving as soon as they can find a replacement...'

Sean stepped forward and caught hold of her arm. 'Emma, this is ridiculous! For heaven's sake, hear me out! You're putting words into my mouth. I never expected you to have lived like a nun before I met you!'

She pulled her arm away. 'It's better this way,' she said bitterly. 'The Fulford family has caused enough unhappiness to the people it's touched—we seem to have a knack for it, don't you agree? Now's the time to leave. How could you ever love someone like me?'

There was a despairing little sob in Emma's voice. She gave him a final tormented look and, shutting the door behind her, marched unseeingly down the corridor, tears blinding her eyes.

The cafeteria had been transformed for the evening—balloons hung from the ceiling and on a makeshift platform at one end a bank of lights flashing various colours fronted the turntables of a disco. A large crowd of staff was piling into the room. Bill was a popular and highly regarded nurse and everyone was anxious to give him a good send-off at his retirement party.

Emma stood with Tania and Connie, trying to forget that her feet were killing her and that she really wasn't in a party mood. Since breaking up with Sean, she'd felt empty and sad, her thoughts continually returning to what might have been. She hoped against hope that he wouldn't be coming or, if he was, that she could slip away fairly soon.

'You look terrific, Emma,' said Tania admiringly. 'I wish I could get into something like that silk suit you're wearing. It would just reveal every bump and lump of adipose tissue I possess!'

'Thank you,' said Emma gloomily. 'I don't feel terrific. I think most of the population of Carrfield came to Casualty today!'

'Have a swig of this wonderful Chateau Sludge from the hospital cellars,' said Bob, thrusting a glass in her hand. 'It'll help to numb the feeling of complete exhaustion.'

They all laughed and Emma looked round at them affectionately. They were good people to work with and she would miss them when she left. She would tell the hospital administrator that she wanted to leave as soon as he could get someone to replace her—it was after all only a locum position so she would have had to have looked for something else eventually.

The banging of a gavel on a table gradually silenced everyone, and one of the consultants strode onto the platform to make a presentation to Bill. His speech was rather long and rambling and Emma's attention wandered, her gaze flicking over the assembled crowd. She was vaguely surprised at how different everyone looked out of hospital garb. She didn't notice a tall figure come up to their group and stand just behind her.

Formalities eventually over, and a beaming Bill having been presented with a voucher and an enormous garden seat, the consultant stepped forward to the microphone once again.

'And now let battle commence! Everyone on the dance floor—but no injuries, please. Remember most of the casualty staff are *not* on duty at the moment!'

A sudden barrage of sound reverberated around the room as the disco started up, and a large proportion of the crowd leapt into action with enthusiasm. Bob swept Connie off to dance, and Zak and Tania began a complicated routine with some other staff. Emma felt a hand on her shoulder.

'I think we're expected to dance,' said a deep voice.

Emma whirled round to see Sean looking quizzically down at her. He was wearing a white shirt, open at the neck, and jeans, and looked cool even in the steamy atmosphere of the disco. Her pulse rate went up a few notches and she felt a horrible despair within her. She had no claim on Sean now, and it would be unbearable to dance with him. Unbearable because that wonderful athletic body would be so close to her, torturing her with memories of their love-making.

'I don't think so, Sean,' she said quickly. 'Not a good idea.'

'It would look very odd if we didn't,' he said firmly. 'People would notice if the registrars weren't talking or dancing with each other.'

'Don't be silly,' Emma said lightly. 'As if anyone would be watching us! I certainly don't want you to feel you have to do a duty dance with me.'

'Is that what you think?' His expression was stern, unreadable. 'That to dance with you would be a duty?'

She gave an embarrassed shrug and didn't reply.

Sean looked down at her intently. 'You say you're going to leave, so perhaps we'll call it a farewell dance.' His face twisted into a wry smile. 'The last dance perhaps?'

He took her hand and led her onto the heaving dance floor and put his arm round her waist, drawing her to him and resting his cheek against hers. They were so close she could smell the faint scent of soap on him, feel the throb of his heart beating against her breast and his long lean legs moving with hers. It was torture trying to ignore the almost electrical response of her body, trying to pretend that she felt nothing at all when every natural reaction was to wind her arms round him, lose herself in him.

Emma moved her head and flicked a surreptitious look at Sean as if to imprint for ever his image on her mind—his intelligent, sexy blue eyes and his strong, mobile mouth, the way his dark hair flopped over his forehead—and just a mere inch away from her…

She closed her eyes and wondered if she was completely insane to throw away everything they'd had between them. Then she stiffened her resolve. No good expecting Sean to commit himself to a woman who'd admitted having an affair with a married man…better to part while he still had a little regard for her. She tried to ignore his breath on her cheek, the way his hand had pulled her so close to him that they might have been welded together.

The lights had been dimmed and now there were just flickering lanterns lit on the walls. How beautiful Emma was, thought Sean with an ache in his throat as he watched her face in the shadowy light. Her eyes were closed, long lashes fanned over faintly flushed cheeks, her full lips slightly parted. Her body under the dark blue silk trouser suit felt curvy and sexy, driving him mad with longing. If only she'd believe him when he said that he loved her no matter what her father had done—no matter what she had done in the past. He sighed as they swayed together, their bodies in harmony. They could be so happy together if only Emma could let go her guilt and forget her past demons. She was all he wanted and needed and it was killing him to let her go.

The music had slowed down to a languid beat. It seemed natural to lean against each other, and for a while it seemed to Emma that there were only two of them in the room and the rest of the world had disappeared. Remember this, she told herself, always remember this. Then the lights went up again and the music stopped. Slowly, sadly Emma came back to reality and Sean led her by the hand to a table where the rest of her friends were sitting.

'Anyone want a drink?' asked Sean. 'I'll get a fresh supply of this plonk.'

He walked off to the bar area and Tania leant near to Emma. 'You looked as if you were getting on very well,' she whispered. 'Is everything OK now?'

Emma shook her head. 'I wish,' she sighed. 'That was a sort of goodbye dance, I'm afraid.'

'Why on earth? You love him, he looks crazy about you, for heaven's sake.' Tania shook her head in puzzlement. 'What's gone wrong?'

'That's just it, Tania. I'm afraid Sean isn't all that mad about me—I think I've fallen in his estimation and that's no good for a long-term commitment.'

'What tosh—I don't believe you!'

'It's true—and to make it easier I'm giving in my notice this week. It…it's unbearable working with him and knowing what he must think of me, so I'm putting my cottage back on the market and probably going back near London.'

Tania stared at Emma with astonished eyes. 'You're leaving? That's awful—what will we do without you? Oh, Emma, I'm sure you're making a big mistake—truly!'

Emma leaned forward and gave Tania a hug. 'You're such a good friend,' she whispered. 'I shall miss you horribly. Before I go, we'll have lunch together—we mustn't lose touch.'

She picked up her handbag and waved at everyone round the table. 'Must go,' she said gaily. 'I'm on early tomorrow even if you lot aren't!'

Weaving his way back through the room with the wine, Sean watched Emma leave. He couldn't believe that during that dance he had probably held her in his arms for the last time.

Emma drove slowly back to the cottage, her mind replaying her dance with Sean and the bitter-sweet feelings it evoked. She had really thought that this time she'd found the right man, someone she could share the rest of her life with—it was Sod's law that the past should have come back to haunt her, an irony that Mike Lawton should destroy her happiness twice!

As she parked the car in the little parking bay off the road she could hear Rocket, Sean's dog, barking loudly. She paused for a second when she'd locked the door. It was unusual to hear him bark and she wondered if he was all right. She crossed the little path that ran between the two cottages and peeped through the Sean's sitting-room window. Rocket had his feet up on the sill and was still whining, as if something had disturbed him.

'It's all right, Rocket,' she called through the window. 'Sean will be back soon—calm down!'

The dog pricked up his ears when he heard her voice, then lumbered down from the sill and after prowling round the room for a minute eventually curled up on the floor and put his head on his paws. He seemed to be quite settled again and Emma walked slowly back to her cottage, bleakly thinking about a future without Sean. She was totally unprepared when a figure jumped out from the dark porch and grabbed her round the waist.

She gave a scream of terror and a hand was clamped over her mouth.

'Keep still, you little bitch, and you won't get hurt,' rasped a voice in her ear. 'Open the door quickly—you and I have a little talking to do!'

Numb with shock, her shaking fingers found the key in her bag and managed to put the key in the lock. Her assailant bundled her through the door and pushed her onto the sofa. He was wearing a baggy black track suit and a balaclava covered his face.

'Who…who are you?' Emma managed to croak out. 'What do you want?'

The man chuckled. 'Let's say I'm a friend of your brother's, shall we? A very good friend who doesn't want to see him harmed.'

Emma's mouth was dry, she could hardly swallow. 'Why should he be harmed?' she whispered.

'Because he owes some of us money—we need a little more interest on what he paid us, and I think you're the one to help us out of his little difficulty!

You see, we've been watching him rather closely and we know when he's needed help you've been a tower of strength to him.'

Emma's heart plummeted. Charles had truly got himself into a mess—he hadn't been fooling when he'd told her the people he owed were thugs.

She tried to keep calm, control her breathing. 'You followed him to the hospital, then?'

'We were just keeping an eye on him.'

'He's paid you what he owes you, hasn't he? I've no more money to pay out anyway…'

'Oh, I think you can manage something, darlin'. You're a doctor, aren't you? Earning quite a bit, I imagine. Anyway, if I can't persuade you to help him, perhaps he could ask you himself!'

He backed to the door, keeping his eyes on Emma and shouted out, 'Bring him in, Jacko—his little sister's here and longing to see him!'

There was the sound of a scuffle outside and a moan of agony as a man stumbled through the door, his hands tied behind his back and blood seeping from a wound on his head.

'Charles! Oh, my God, what have they done to you?' Emma stared in horror at her brother as he swayed across the floor and crashed onto one of the chairs.

'I'm all right, sis,' he said thickly. 'I've given them what I owed them, but the swine have come back for more.' He turned a desperate face to her. 'I'm sorry, Emma, this has all got out of control. I never thought it would end like this…'

His head flopped back against the cushions of the chair and he closed his eyes. Emma heard him murmur faintly, 'Don't give in to them, Emma…'

There were two men in the room now—the second man, Jacko, was swarthy and thick-set, his face uncovered. They sat down on either side of Charles, and Jacko grinned at Emma.

'You can see the situation, can't you, Doctor? If you don't come up with a cheque for two thousand pounds in a few minutes, you may have to give some treatment to your brother here. If you're co-operative we won't outstay our welcome and he won't get hurt!'

Emma felt her terror begin to subside and blind fury suddenly took over. How often had she had to deal with thugs like these in Casualty? Usually their aggression was drug- or alcohol-induced—these men seemed totally sober and to be enjoying their sadistic antics. She clenched her teeth. She damn well wouldn't be intimidated by them—she would play them along and hope that at some stage she could escape and get some help.

'I'll have to get my cheque book,' she hedged. 'And, of course, it will probably bounce. I don't keep that kind of money in my account.'

'You write it out, darlin'. You can go to the bank tomorrow and make arrangements. They won't refuse a doctor a loan, I'm sure!' snarled one of the men. 'If the cheque bounces, we'll be back!'.

Emma shot a look at her brother. He was lying back in the chair, his face deathly pale, the blood seeping down his face a dull red.

'Give my brother some water,' she said in a steely voice. 'I don't know what injuries he's sustained in your attack—but if he dies, you could be up on a murder charge!'

The swarthy man laughed. 'He's only been tickled!

Next time it could be more serious... Now, get up and get that cheque book—and I'm coming with you!'

Emma rose slowly to her feet, trying to work out a way to let the outside world know she was in trouble. Then she and the man walked to the kitchen and she switched on the light, then switched it off again, trying to do it as if flashing a morse signal for SOS.

'What the hell are you doing?' The man's hand slashed across her face, almost knocking her into the cooker. 'Don't try any funny business—just get the cheque!'

Emma stumbled to the dresser drawer, her cheek numb where the man had hit her. She pulled out the cheque book then, with the man close behind her, walked back to the sitting room. Just as she was about to sit down there was a sound of frantic barking and whining outside the front door.

Rocket! Emma's heart leapt in hope, wondering how he'd got out of Sean's house and if anyone would take any notice of his barking. Then there was a tremendous bang and the front door flew open, splintered from the outside by a hefty kick. In a second the room was filled with several shouting policeman, two grabbing hold of the men, another blocking the doorway, and in their wake bounded Rocket, closely followed by Sean!

For a minute it seemed chaotic. Yells and obscenities filled the air and Emma crouched by Charles's side until the police had the two men under control. Then she felt herself being hauled up to her feet, two arms went round her waist and Sean was gazing at her as if he would never let her out of his sight again.

'What the hell did you get yourself into?' he said,

devouring her face with his eyes. 'Are you all right, sweetheart? Did they hurt you?'

And then Emma broke down, the strain of the last half-hour finally breaking her control, and she clung to him desperately. 'Sean…I didn't realise what was happening. They completely took me by surprise and when they threatened to injure Charles again, I felt so helpless!'

'It's all right now,' he soothed, stroking her hair and cuddling her to him. 'The bastards have been well and truly caught, and I hope they get the book thrown at them.'

'What…what about Charles?'

'We've called for an ambulance and as far as I can see the head wound is reasonably superficial. He's not in danger.'

Emma drew in a big shuddering sigh. 'I can't believe it,' she said shakily. 'How did you know what was happening and get here so quickly?'

'Because I followed you after the disco—I couldn't let what we had just disappear. I thought if I talked to you at home I'd be able to persuade you that I really meant it when I said I loved you.'

'You followed me? So you saw me being attacked?'

'No—I didn't realise what had happened at first. But luckily I thought I'd take Rocket for a quick walk before I came to your cottage and he made like a homing pigeon for your front door, barking his head off. I thought something weird was going on and called the police on my mobile. Some instinct told me it might be something to do with your brother, although I never dreamed it would be something as bad as this.'

He touched the scarlet mark on her cheek where the

man had hit her. 'Poor darling,' he whispered. 'I'd like to do something pretty radical to the scum that did this to you.'

'Good old Rocket!' breathed Emma. 'If you hadn't come in when you did…'

'But I did.' Sean grinned, sliding his arms around her again and moving his head towards hers, kissing her gently at first, then with increased passion, moving his lips over her jawline and neck. And she didn't resist, allowing herself to succumb to his fervour and comforted by his loving touch.

One of the policemen coughed discreetly behind them. 'Er…excuse me, sir, we're taking these two off now—they're under arrest—and the paramedics would like a word with you regarding Mr Fulford. When you've a minute,' he added with a twinkle in his eye.

Charles had been taken outside and was being lifted into the ambulance. Emma held his hand and smiled down at his stricken, ravaged face.

'You'll be OK, Charles. I'll be in to see you tomorrow.' She paused and said gently, 'Does Mum know anything about this?'

'No—she was looking after Ben. As far as she knows, I just went out to meet some friends.'

'Some friends,' remarked Emma drily.

'I'm so sorry, little sis,' he croaked. 'Believe me, I've learned my lesson. I can't tell you how guilty I feel that you were dragged into all this. I seem to have had a period of complete madness, but I'll make it up to you, I promise. You do believe me, don't you?'

He looked up at her anxiously and she bent down and kissed his cheek.

'Yes, I truly believe you. Now you can start life again with a clean slate.'

He squeezed her hand and a faint smile appeared on his lips. 'Looks like you're making a new start, too—I always thought Sean Casey was more than a colleague!'

Emma flicked away the hair from her eyes, about to deny that Sean meant anything more to her than a workmate. Then she smiled and said softly, 'Perhaps he is—I'm not quite sure yet.'

She glanced over towards Sean, who was having a word with the paramedics. He was so dependable, so wonderful and lovable—just why was she trying to get away from him? Perhaps he really did still feel something for her? Would he have kissed her like he had a moment ago if he hadn't wanted to be with her, or had it been done in the heat of the rescue?

Emma watched the ambulance drive off, then turned back to the cottage with a sigh—the last thing she wanted to do was sleep there that night. She supposed she would go back to her mother's and hoped she wouldn't enquire too deeply why she wasn't spending the night in her own house or why Charles wasn't home.

'I don't know where you're wandering off to,' said Sean, coming up to her and taking her arm. 'You're coming back with me, Emma—no argument!'

'Would that be wise?' she murmured, but she didn't resist him.

He didn't reply but propelled her back along the path to his cottage. The moon was out, a silver disc in the velvety sky, and the stars were myriad sparkling jewels arching above them. On the beach the sea was calm, just the gentle swooshing of waves on the sand.

They stood for a moment looking at the tranquil scene, the faint smell of the sea mingled with sweet grass wafting over towards them. Sean pulled Emma down on the velvety, mossy grass just before the shoreline and took her hands in his.

'Emma Fulford,' he said slowly, 'I want to make one thing very clear—I love you, with all my heart and soul. I didn't want to at first—after all, you were your father's daughter! But then I realised that you were what I had been looking for all my life and I'm not going to let you go now. You and I aren't going to pay for the mistakes of our parents!'

She looked at him solemnly, her tawny eyes large and dark in the moonlight. 'What about my mistakes, Sean?'

'Believe me, we've all made mistakes in our past—we've all got baggage we bring with us. You seemed to carry a large amount of guilt with you, but in my opinion the guilty one was Mike. He was the one who lied to you, who betrayed his wife. He was nothing but a con man, determined to have everything he wanted, whatever harm it did to anyone else.'

'I was a fool,' Emma sighed.

He tilted her face to his and brushed her lips with his. 'I know one thing, my love, when you marry me, that won't be a mistake. It'll be the wisest thing we've ever done.'

Emma leant away from him for a moment and stared into his clear eyes. 'Marry you? You want me to marry you?'

'Is that so awful a prospect?' he teased. 'People do

still marry each other, you know! Are you going to remain single all your life just because of one mistake?'

And suddenly Emma laughed, a light-hearted sound that bubbled out of her, filled with happiness. If Sean was prepared to forget about the past, why shouldn't she?

'You know,' she said, touching his lips with her finger and looking at him teasingly. 'After our drive together in the taxi on my first day at Carrfield, you were the last person I wanted to see again! I couldn't believe that we would have to work together!'

'And now?' he said, arching one eyebrow.

She flung her arms round him and kissed him softly. 'Now, my darling Dr Casey, I think being married to you would be very like heaven!'

'Heaven indeed,' murmured Sean.

'We've got a lot of time to make up,' he murmured, turning towards her. 'So let's start now, my darling...'

Then he lay on the grass and pulled her down next to him beside the lapping waves and the whispering sands.